Miss Bertie Explains
the Beginning of the World

Miss Bertie Explains the Beginning of the World

Minnie Lamberth

MINNIE LAMBERTH BOOKS
MONTGOMERY, ALABAMA

Copyright 2020 by Minnie Lamberth

ISBN 978-0-9855883-2-8

Cover and interior design by Slats Slaton

Published by Minnie Lamberth
Montgomery, Alabama
http://minnielamberth.com

For Anne and Jane,
my favorite daughters
of Wessobulga

"Sing, barren woman, you who never bore a child; burst into song, shout for joy, you who were never in labor; because more are the children of the desolate woman than of her who has a husband," says the LORD.

– *Isaiah 54:1 (NIV)*

CONTENTS

The Revelation Awaits

Wellton, Alabama
September 1995

Rain was coming down in buckets as the new reporter for *The Wellton Courier* sloshed her way through the parking lot on her first day on the job. With a sizeable purse over her shoulder, she opened the lobby door with one hand while juggling in the other a wayward umbrella that blew inside out as she entered the building. Once inside, however, she negotiated the umbrella to a close, took a breath and exhaled.

"See?" she told herself. "It's not too late to make a good first impression." Except that in the next moment, she moved forward, and the squeak of soaked shoes seemed to grow louder with each step she took across the tile floor. By then, she'd caught the attention of a lanky gentleman standing at the counter.

"Hannah Hayes? That you?" Earl Ford crooked his neck, as if unsure of his theory.

"The one and only," Hannah said as she pushed back a strand of wet hair stuck to her face.

"My mom told me you were back in town." Earl and Hannah's brother had been neighborhood friends as kids.

"What brings you to the newsroom?" she asked.

"Getting a classified ad."

"Not in the personals, I hope?" Hannah said teasingly.

"Naw, girl. Amber would kill me if I did that. It's for my old fishing boat. It's ugly, but it does the job. You interested? I can cut you a deal."

"I'll pass, but thanks."

Motioning to the lobby window, Earl said, "With all this rain, I probably ought to upgrade it for an ark."

"Good idea."

"So, how's Franklin?" he asked.

"He's doing well. He's up in Huntsville working for a technology company. He and Betty have a six-year-old son and a four-year-old daughter."

"Cool. So what about you, girl?" Earl gave a wink. "If it keeps raining, you got somebody to enter the ark with?"

"Ha," Hannah said as she remembered now that Earl was a flirt. "Not at the moment. I'm just home for a while. I'm taking some time to write."

"About what?"

"I don't know," she shrugged. "I guess I'll figure that out when I figure it out."

"Well, alright, girl," Earl said. "You tell your momma I said hey."

"I will."

CHAPTER 1

The Word Goes Fourth

A half-dozen first graders pulled their chairs into a semi-circle around the ancient teacher who had surely been teaching these lessons since Gutenberg was a baby. Miss Bertie's white hair was pulled up in a bun. Her bifocals rested lopsided on her nose. Her print dress draped loosely around her expansive figure, and puffy ankles protruded just beyond the sensible black shoes she laced over knee-high stockings.

"Settle down, children," Miss Bertie said. "It's time to listen to a story from the Bible."

As the class waited expectantly, Miss Bertie read three words out loud: "In the beginning." Then she paused and looked above the fingerprint smudges on her lenses toward her young class members.

"Now," she announced into the room. "Children, I have just read to you the most famous three words in all the world, over all time. 'In the beginning.' If you said these three words, in this order, to pretty much anyone you meet today, he or she will know exactly where the words came from, and where they belong."

Miss Bertie paused to let the children's little brains catch up to her sentences. Also, she felt as if a burp was coming up from that second cup of coffee she should not have consumed. As she pressed on her chest to suppress any errant bodily noise, she cleared her throat and kept going.

"In the beginning. Let's say these words together."

"In the beginning," the class repeated. Not surprisingly, the words came out like a record skipping on a turntable (which you may not have ever heard unless you yourself are very old). "In in in the the the beginning beginning beginning" the class actually said as the various little voices tried unsuccessfully to keep pace with their teacher and each other.

Miss Bertie continued, "Most of the people you will ever meet over the rest of your lifetimes will know that these three words are the start of the Bible. That's how famous 'in the beginning' is. They are in the first verse of the first chapter of the Bible's first book—Genesis 1:1."

As Miss Bertie looked down to her notes, she said with mock surprise, "Now, let's see here. It appears that after these three very famous words, there's another one. Can any of you tell me what the fourth word of the Bible is?"

The children, being children and not very responsive to word-count scenarios or otherwise obtuse questions, offered only blank looks. Thus, Miss Bertie answered her own question, just as she had intended.

"Children, I'm here to tell you, you'll remember the first three words of the Bible for as long as you're able to remember. Yet there's a word that comes next—a Name … the Creator and Author of the story … the One who spoke this world into being. The fourth word is the one you must not forget. Because what this word in the story tells you is that God was already here … in the beginning."

Miss Bertie's voice lifted into the room and fell toward the little listening ears. What any of them would do with this piece of information, however, remained to be seen.

Miss Bertie continued, "You know how, when you woke up this morning, the day had already started? It was already here? You didn't have to hang the sun in the sky or put the moon in the closet, correct?"

The children giggled slightly at the thought of arranging the celestial bodies each morning. "All of that was done for you, right?" Miss Bertie continued. "Someone, Something, was here before you joined this day, before you joined the story. And if you go back and back and back all through time, you'll find that Someone was God. 'In the beginning God' that's how the Bible actually begins. 'In the beginning God created the heavens and the earth.'"

Miss Bertie cleared her throat as she let these words settle in the small classroom located within Wellton Baptist Church in Wellton, Alabama, in September 1995. For too many years to count, she'd been coming to this church to teach children on Sundays, and here she was again.

"Now," she said. Like a hand clap or glass clink, she threw out that word to focus her audience's attention. "Children, when grown-ups tell a story, they try to answer six questions: who, what, when, where, why, and how. The Bible begins with most of the answers to a very big story. They're right there in the first verse. 'In the beginning God created the heavens and the earth.' That tells us the Who and what. God is the Who. Created the heavens and earth is what He did. Some people over time have concerned themselves greatly with the When. They can argue quite strongly about it, I assure you. For now we'll just say 'in the beginning.' Where is right here. Right here on Planet Earth."

Miss Bertie looked to her little class members as she said gently, "Dearies, the Why is the sting. The testing ground. The unknown. The three-letter question that will follow us around like our own shadow on a summer day, or a gnat at a picnic that can't be batted away. For now, we have to take 'why' out of the story and place it in a box called faith. Or trust, if you prefer. We trust that God had a good reason for all He has done or allowed."

As Miss Bertie scanned the faces of her class for curious and/or confused expressions, her eyes landed on a girl whose head was tilted to the side, arms crossed.

"Emily," Miss Bertie inquired, "have you ever asked your parents why you cannot do something you want to do, only to have them answer 'because I said so?'"

Emily nodded thoughtfully. "Yes, ma'am."

"Well, hold on to that thought, and I'll get back to it. So, 'why' is something we will all have to find the answer for later. But the 'how' has already been answered. We know how God did it. We know how He created the world."

Miss Bertie paused for a second before shifting her voice toward a pleasant lightness, the same she'd use when asking if anyone wanted juice and crackers. "Children, would you like to know how God created the world?"

Most of the children nodded in the affirmative, though one boy said a southern "yaheeesss" that stretched on for quite a bit.

"God looked out into this great big nothingness—where there was no sky, no land, no air to breathe, and no people to breathe the air that wasn't there. There was no sound—not a voice, not a laugh, not a cry, not a bird's chirp, not an animal's growl. To see what He saw and heard, you'd have to be wearing the tightest blindfold ever with earplugs to boot."

From the side of her mouth, Miss Bertie blew back a strand of white hair that had fallen from her bun, then she said, "Into this emptiness that was darker and quieter than any of us can imagine, God spoke four words: 'Let there be light.'

"Children, I am here to tell you, God created light with His very voice. He spoke the world into existence. He spoke the daytime and nighttime into their schedules. He spoke the land and the sea into their positions. He spoke the plants and trees into the earth, and he spoke the creatures of the earth into being. By His words, these things happened."

Miss Bertie's voice grew quiet, as if revealing a pet theory. "Children, you might think of these creative actions as the divine version of 'because I said so.' Because for God, that's all it took."

"Now," Miss Bertie said, returning to her strong voice. "After God created the world, He turned His attention to something that was even more important than anything He had done so far. He said, 'Let us make man in our own image.' It was time for people to enter the world and take their place in creation."

Miss Bertie went back to that voice of quiet theorizing. "Children, I don't know if you notice what just happened here, but all of a sudden in this story, God goes from 'said' to 'make.' Let's think about that for a moment. Let's think about the difference between these two sentences: I am going to say something. I am going to make something."

Miss Bertie pointed a finger to her mouth as she asked, "If you say something, what do you use?"

The finger prompt is presumably why the class knew to yell out, "Your mouth!"

Then Miss Bertie held out her hands as if she were holding an unseen object. "Now, if I say, 'I am going to make something, what do you think I will use?"

"Your hands!" the class yelled out.

Miss Bertie nodded with solemn satisfaction. "Yes, children. God said, 'Let us make man in our own image,' and you can almost hear in this word 'make' that He got His hands involved. We have, each one of us, been touched by God, by His tender love and care. His hand was on our lives then and is on our lives to this day, even to this very moment."

Miss Bertie glanced toward the classroom door. Through the small window above the handle, she could see parental faces starting to gather. With her time nearly up, she presented her concluding statement: "Children, that is how the world began."

A father tapped on the door as he pulled it open. "Emily," his voice boomed in mock whisper, "we've got to get rolling. Grab your Bible and let's go." With a glance toward the teacher, he offered a sincere tone delivered with crisp enunciation to say, "Pardon my interruption, Miss Bertie, we've got to be somewhere."

Indeed they did. Emily's dad was the "Voice of the Family," the one who spoke his words into the world every Sunday afternoon from 2 p.m. – 4 p.m. during a call-in show on the local radio station. Whether Mark Daniel was on the air or in the hallway, he had a habit of saying "ahh" or "hmm" or "I see" with a certain flair. Radio people usually fill the silence. This time, however, Mark paused for a long look back into the classroom, past the children and landing on the teacher, as if evaluating an unspoken concern.

CHAPTER 2

Calling the Committee to Order

The next Wednesday, a group of men and women gathered at the Wellton Baptist Church to discuss a potential issue. They'd brought their trays of church supper into a room just off the fellowship hall, where Clyde Buchanan, a CPA in a suit, presented the situation as best he knew it.

"This couple came by my house and they were asking questions, such as did I go to church. If not, why don't I go to church. They asked things like, what would make church more comfortable? What if the music were more modern, like a rock band? The woman asked, what if I could wear anything I wanted? It was just weird."

The committee members murmured in agreement about the weirdness of the questions.

Clyde shook his head as he said, "I mean, I thought I was about to sign up for a time-share. This was serious business about meeting my needs. Since when is church about meeting my needs?"

"Amen, brother," Sam Prichard said, affirming Clyde's apprehension. Though the truth is, Sam Prichard usually said "amen, brother" to most things being discussed.

Clyde nodded at the acknowledgment and continued, "What I found out later was that this was an 'advance team' for something called The Eternal Rock Community Church. They've been looking at that old building off Piedmont, thinking they can fill it up with some chairs, microphones, and amplifiers and call it a church." Clyde shook his head. "But basically they're going to be playing loud rock music, wearing jeans, and doing who knows what all else."

"Hmm," Mark Daniel said in radio-suitable voice as he tried to bring the point home with carefully enunciated words. "Church is becoming entertainment? Is that what I'm hearing?"

"Exactly right," Clyde said.

Mark took over the discussion. "Well, I appreciate that we're called to reach people 'where they are' and create inviting environments that will draw people in. But there's something to be said for making church different from our regular lives. I think we need to know we're at church, and that includes wearing something decent, singing hymns with the congregation, and listening to a message from the pastor that brings it home. We need to be able to get a word from the Word that we can take with us."

"Amen, brother," Sam said.

"I mean, this is just my opinion, obviously," Mark quickly added.

"Yes, of course," Clyde echoed. "These are just our opinions that they're not doing it right. The Lord works in mysterious ways. But our charge, really, is to make sure this church is strong. That's why we're meeting. Our goal is not to stop other people from expressing their call any way they see fit but to make sure we're doing our best for the Lord right here. So, with that in mind, we need to analyze where we are. In the business world, we do that with a S.W.O.T. analysis—an evaluation of our strengths, weaknesses, opportunities, and threats. So let's start with our strengths."

Clyde stood to write on the chalkboard as committee members enthusiastically offered extensive examples on the plus side of things. Committee secretary Maggie

Johnson dutifully recorded the strengths in a notebook, however, for a more permanent record.

When Clyde got to "weaknesses," the committee members racked their brains but finally came up with a few teeny tiny issues they were experiencing as areas where they could do better. The call for "opportunities" brought back the enthusiasm. Then they got to "threats."

That's when Mark asked the question that had been gnawing at him for some time. "Folks, is our children's department where it needs to be? If we're going to grow and sustain a church, we do that by drawing young families. That's what the research shows. So, if there's any area where we can lose out to a place that makes church fun and exciting, it's going to be there."

"Amen, brother," Sam Prichard said.

"And ... I mean ... so what you've got in the children's department right there in first grade ... well, I'm wondering if this may be a situation that needs attention." Mark paused as he tried to find the words. "You know ... Elijah had Elisha ... Moses had Joshua ... David had Solomon." After citing these biblical examples of transitions in leadership, he added, "There's a time and season for everything, and sometimes we need to make a change for the good of the church, for the good of our people."

"Amen, brother," said Sam.

Myra Hamilton, who'd served as head of Children's Sunday School for going on forty years, asked a question of clarification. "Mark, are you trying to make, shall we say, a delicate point about Bertie Dupree? Are you wanting to move her out of the department?"

"Well, not 'out' so much as just moved to a different role, perhaps—something more suitable for this season, you might say. God bless her, but I'm not even sure she can see through the smudges in her glasses. When I drop my Emily off in that room, it just gives me pause."

Myra was a large boned woman who struck an imposing presence, especially with a heavily sprayed and unmoving helmet of jet black hair that was just as dark as it had ever been. It could be said that welcoming input about areas under her purview was not exactly her spiritual gift. "Has there been an incident?" Myra asked pointedly.

"No, thank the Lord," Mark answered. "Not as far as I know, but what if something did happen? I think the question must be asked, is she really at a place where she can take care of these kids?" Mark shrugged. "Like I said, even Elijah had Elisha."

"All I know is this," Myra said. "She's been our most faithful teacher for too many years to count, and it's hard to get teachers to make that kind of commitment Sunday after Sunday. If we move her out, who moves in?"

The committee sat silently for a moment. Then Clyde turned to Maggie Johnson, "Let's put down 'children's department' as an area where we should give some attention. This is, after all, a brainstorming session. It's not the time to solve problems, but just a chance to see where we are."

CHAPTER 3

Animals Get Their Names

So the Case of the Rock Church and the Old Lady was already under evaluation when a half-dozen first graders gathered the next Sunday for another lesson.

"Settle down, class," Miss Bertie said to the group of children who had assembled in six chairs in front of the oversized teacher in a floral print dress and sensible shoes. "It's time to hear a story from the Bible."

Miss Bertie told how God had made and placed Adam, the first man, in the Garden of Eden, then she segued to another point. "Now, God had made all the wild animals too, but there was an issue," she said. "None of these animals had any names. Imagine that you saw an elephant but didn't know what to call it, or if you saw a dog but didn't know it was a dog. God brought all of the animals to Adam so that he could give them names."

Miss Bertie looked out to her class. "Do any of you have, let's say, a stuffed animal?"

The hand of a quiet student rose in the air. "I have a lot of stuffed animals," Millie offered in a soft voice.

"Millie, did you give these stuffed animals names?" Miss Bertie asked.

"Un huh, there's Silly Willy and Claire Bear and Sweet Pea and …"

"Well, those are all very nice names," Miss Bertie said as she held up a hand to wrap up the stuffed animal roll call. "Now, to give something a name is a great responsibility. A name tells you what something is, or what you think it is. A name is not just calling a person Cynthia or Billy or Brad. If you say something is smart or dumb or good or bad, you are also giving it a name. Sometimes we give people nicknames—some of which are funny or sweet, but some aren't very nice, right?"

Emily raised her hand as she said, "A boy in my neighborhood called me Poopy Face one time." Classmate Christopher laughed out loud and repeated "Poopy Face" as Miss Bertie held up her hand again.

"Emily, I bet you didn't think that was very nice," she said. Emily shook her head no.

"Now, I think I should point out," Miss Bertie continued, "the list of names that Adam gave the animals is not in the Bible. It's not which names he gave them that's important. If Adam had called an elephant a dog, or an alligator a cat, we'd be fine with that. We'd just call them whatever we knew their names to be. But what is important is that God gave people the ability to give names to things. And we should use this ability with great care—so that we won't hurt each other. Because if you give something a name, God is watching what name you give it."

Miss Bertie cleared her throat as she tried to hide a burp from the children. Maybe, she surmised, she really was getting too old for that second cup of coffee.

"In any case, Adam was on the earth with a lot of animals, but none of these animals were the right kind of helper for him. God felt someone else would be more suitable, so He put Adam into a deep sleep, took one of His ribs, and fashioned a new type of person called Woman. He named her Eve, and there they were—Adam and Eve in the Garden of Eden.

"Now, one of the beautiful things about being in this

garden is that these first people felt no shame or embarrassment, not the least little bit. Do you ever feel bad about something you've said or done, or do you ever feel bad about how a parent or teacher has corrected you after you've messed up?"

The children nodded yes.

"Well, this was before any of that kind of feeling had ever happened. At this moment in the history of the earth, no one had ever felt bad about anything. So far, it's just a beautiful story of God creating the world. Then something goes wrong."

Miss Bertie moved on to the part of the story about how God had said it was okay to eat from any tree in the garden except for one. Yet a serpent came along with a tempting idea about eating the fruit from this very tree. "Well, children, I bet you know what happens next."

"Eve ate the apple," Christopher said.

"So did Adam," Emily added.

"Yes, and they felt shame about having done something that God didn't want them to do. Now, when they heard God calling, they hid from His voice, but not for long— because God found them and talked with them about what had happened. So it was decision time. Because the man and woman could have stretched out their hands and taken from the tree of life to live forever, God removed them from the garden and placed them instead in another part of the earth where they would work and raise a family."

Miss Bertie noticed a face peering anxiously through the window in the door. Millie's mom, a thin and nervous lady in her mid-20s, eased quietly into the room and stood in the corner behind the backs of the six children.

Miss Bertie concluded her lesson. "I think it's important to see that this situation is not entirely about punishment. When Adam and Eve felt shame, they had covered their bodies with fig leaves, but God went a step better than that. God took care of them by making their clothes. Have you ever had anyone sew clothes for you?"

Millie nodded with vigor. "My mom sews clothes for me," she said.

"Yes, and when she does that, she is doing what God did Himself for the very first people. When she sews clothes for you, dearie, your mom is doing the Lord's work. Isn't that delightful?"

Millie beamed at this affirmation and happily nodded again. Millie's mom's face grew pink as well as she broke into an unexpected smile herself.

"Now, children, I see that your parents are gathering, and it's time for you to go," Miss Bertie concluded. "But our separation will not be for long because we will be back together again next week."

Just then, Mark Daniel's voice boomed into the room. "Emily, come on, sweetie. It's time to get to church. Tell Miss Bertie thank you for teaching you this morning."

Emily reached to hug Miss Bertie goodbye as her dad spoke to the elderly teacher. "We appreciate all you do for the church, Miss Bertie. You've sure been at this a while, haven't you?"

"Not hardly a minute, son. Not hardly a minute," Miss Bertie responded. "Like the scripture says, there's little to no difference between an hour and a thousand years. So I'd say I'm just barely getting started. You have a good week, dear."

Mark nodded with great solemnity. "Same to you, Miss Bertie." As he walked away, he began to think through an idea for his afternoon broadcast.

CHAPTER 4

Name Check in the Cereal Aisle

A few hours later, Mark Daniel's call-in show meandered around to the topic, "What if you're holding on too long?" He began with a charming story of how his mom taught him to tie his shoes back when he was a kid, then he punctuated his point with this conclusion: "Friends, let me ask you, what if my mom—bless her heart—kept trying to tie my shoes every day?" He laughed as he added, "I wouldn't have gotten very far, would I? I'd have been telling her, 'Mom, I can do this for myself.' So folks, that's just my way of saying, sometimes it's time to let go, and that's what I'd like to talk about today. Even Elijah had Elisha. The phone lines are open. Give me a call and let's discuss."

A man named Rich called in first to tell the story of how his dad taught him to fish. "At first he put the bait on the hook for me," Rich said. "I didn't want to do it. I didn't want to deal with that squirmy worm. But then one day Dad told me, 'Son, you've got to do it yourself.' And I did. Now I've taught my own boy. If my dad hadn't pushed me into doing it for myself, I wouldn't have been able to pass that knowledge down to my own son."

"Good example, sir. Good example," Mark responded. "We've got another caller on the line. Let's see if he agrees." The show was moving along swimmingly until near the end when a lady called in. "Alright, friends, we've got Carmen on the line," the host said. "Let's see what a womanly point of view can offer about this subject."

The lady's voice spoke with uncertainty. "Hi, can you hear me? Am I on?"

"You're on, Carmen. Go ahead and tell us your thoughts about when it's time to let go."

"Well, I sort of have a different perspective on all of this because I just had a really interesting experience at the Piggly Wiggly, and I think it relates to your topic," Carmen said. "My thought is, you never know who can have an impact on your life whatever age they are."

"Tell us about it," Mark prompted.

"You see, there was this lady leaning down to pick up a container of oatmeal. I say this as gently as I can, but she was of a generous size. I guess I'm a visual person, and out of the corner of my eye, I saw her floral print dress, some black lace-up shoes and these knee-high stockings that were sort of falling down. No disrespect intended, of course."

"Of course," Mark agreed cautiously. "Please continue."

"Anyway, she lifted the oatmeal off the shelf, stood up straight, and when she turned my way, she just started talking. She said, 'Have you ever noticed how we call it a 'box' of oatmeal, but it's really a cylinder?'"

"'No, ma'am, I never noticed that,' I told her.

"So right there in the cereal aisle, this lady started talking about what we call things. She asked me, 'If we call it a box, but it's really a cylinder, do you ever wonder what else we're getting wrong?' I'd never really thought about that, to be honest. Then she told me, 'We have the power to give names to things, but we should be careful what names we give these things—wouldn't you agree?'

"So I said, 'Yeah sure.' I actually didn't know what she was talking about, but she asked in a way where you just say yes to whatever it is. Then she said, 'Especially when we give ourselves names?' And that made me think. So I started telling her about something that was bothering me. It's this phrase 'broken home' that I hear, as if the home I'm in with my daughter is broken. It's just hard to hear that.

"Well, this lady looked straight at me and said, 'Dearie, don't let anyone give your home a name it doesn't deserve.' I have to tell you, I choked up right there in the cereal aisle. Couldn't even speak. But it's made me really think about the names I give things.

"There was something else too, and I remember just how she said it. She said, 'It seems you've been sent out from your comfortable place, and here you are. Now. What will you do during your journey? What will you do with the gifts within?'

"I thought for a moment, a split second really, and the answer just came out: I'm going to start painting. I've always loved art ever since I was a little girl. I actually minored in art in college but didn't pursue it as a career or anything.

"She said, 'Well, dearie, God is our Creator, and when you are creating, you are doing the Lord's work.' So that's what I'm going to do.

"Anyway, thank you for letting me say this. That lady said her name was Miss Bertie. I'll never forget her."

Mark Daniel cleared his throat as he said, "Well, alrighty then. Thank you for calling. Let's see if we've got time for someone else today."

Carmen's call and Mark's response were coming through the radio as Hannah Hayes pulled her Honda Civic into the driveway of her childhood home on Evergreen Drive. Hannah knew Miss Bertie—had known her forever and, in fact, had just driven past the old Dupree house on Southview to get to Evergreen. Having this conversation with Carmen sounded just like something her old Sunday school teacher would do.

"I should go see Miss Bertie while I'm here," Hannah said to herself. "Maybe that would help." She grabbed her purse and a sack from the passenger seat and stepped out of her car.

CHAPTER 5

There's No Place Like Home

World-crashes come in all sizes. Sometimes it's in the death or illness of a parent, sometimes in a relationship break-up, and sometimes in a retreat to a place you said you'd never return. Those were the crashes that brought Hannah Hayes back to Wellton in her thirtieth year.

She walked into a quiet house and stepped into the kitchen where she noticed on the counter a vase of cut flowers and a loaf of banana bread—the latest offerings from friends and neighbors encouraging her mother's recovery. Opening the refrigerator, she moved around a couple of casserole dishes to find a spot for the milk and eggs she'd picked up at the Piggly Wiggly. She turned toward the hallway and, a few steps later, peeked into her mother's room as Mary Hayes opened her eyes.

"Oh. You're back. I was just taking a little nap," Mary said.

"That's fine. I'll be on my computer if you need me."

"Okay, sweetie. But don't stay on the Internet too long. Franklin might call."

"I won't," Hannah replied, reminding herself that, even in moments of trial, some things never change. She had upended life plans to move to town and take a job at *The Wellton Courier* so she could regroup while she helped her mother. But she would certainly want to make sure her brother doesn't have to face a busy signal when he calls home.

Furthermore, whether Mary actually needed help was

a matter of continuing debate. Mostly she'd say, "I'm doing fine. I don't need a thing." But there was the grief of her not too distant widowhood, plus she'd retired from her role as an officer at the Wellton Bank, and cancer treatment is never easy.

Hannah glanced out at her neighborhood through a window in her bedroom. The mix of homes that once held familiar faces in families of various sizes had become a place for empty-nesters, widows or widowers, or unknown couples just starting out. Today only a few were the same as the ones she'd known—or who'd known her.

She turned her attention to her room, zeroing in on a computer with a fat monitor sitting on a desktop hard drive hooked up by a phone line to the World Wide Web. This is where she intended to write her world-changing words. Hannah sat at the desk and powered up the equipment as she thought back to a goodbye from a couple of months ago. When the computer came to life, she opened a new document and began to type.

"I'm leaving," she explained to the young man who was nice in every way, except for that part about a puzzling disregard for a work ethic and too much enjoyment of festive libations.

"Too late, I'm already gone," he said as the door to that chapter closed.

Undeterred, she summoned the chorus of voices that ran through her head, the voices that ignored the posted sign "no running." The computer, that's where you get your strength ... There's something you love more than me though you may not know it. Your computer ... Do you mean to tell me Hannah O'Hara that your computer means nothing to you? Why, it's the only thing worth living for, worth dying for."

The closing scene of Scarlett O'Hara's familiar role had

come back to mind and been moved around for Hannah's own situation. When Scarlett didn't know what else to do, she went home. "Yes, that is the answer," Hannah said to herself. *Look for that place where you are most who you are,* she typed.

She was pleased by her thoughts, and discomforted as well. For someone else, an epic film set on southern plantations may not be entirely appreciated, especially considering that slavery is part of the story. Her fingers stopped typing as she sat still until she found another phrase.

You can't go home again. "That can't possibly be true when clearly I did," she said to herself. "The road is still there. The house is still here. Is it that I have changed?" She typed another phrase.

There's no place like home. "Certainly true," she mused, "in that this collection of factors related to longitude and latitude, physical structure, human occupation, and personal history do not have a duplicate anywhere else. But I notice that the statement itself is neither complimentary nor derogatory. So what do I do with that?"

She typed the phrase, *Give attention to what is here.*

Hannah stared at her screen as a creative anxiety rose up within her, and her thoughts got stuck somewhere deep inside. Then she saved the file under the name "Home," pushed her chair back, and walked away.

CHAPTER 6

The First Family Feud

The next Sunday, a class of seven first graders gathered in a row of small chairs as Miss Bertie asked, "Let's see a show of hands. Do any of you have brothers or sisters?"

Six hands rose quickly. Only Millie was an only child.

"Do you ever fuss or pick on your siblings, or get mad at them for something they've done?"

Six of seven kids nodded yes.

"Well, this story in the Bible is about something bad that happened between two brothers. By this point, Adam and Eve had two sons, Cain and Abel. Abel watched the flocks—the animals that belonged to his family. Cain tilled the ground, growing the fruits and vegetables.

"Now, there came a time when these sons were giving an offering back to God to thank Him for what they'd been given. Cain gave an offering from the fruits he had grown in the ground. For some reason, however, God wasn't especially pleased with this offering."

Miss Bertie held her hands palms up as she shrugged. "The Bible teaches us things we need to learn, but we often have to ask questions about what the lesson actually is. Whether there was something specifically wrong with the offering of fruit, I don't know. But, as we'll see, there was definitely something wrong with Cain's response.

"Now. Abel gave an offering from the best of what he had—the firstborn of his flocks and the fatty part. If you don't understand what that means, think of it as going to a really nice restaurant where someone brings your dad a meal and says, 'This is the best steak we have in this whole restaurant. It's the one that costs the most money and is prepared in the most delicious manner. I want to give it to you.' Your dad would probably be so pleased to receive this gift of a delicious steak.

"But what if, at the same time, someone came along and said, 'Oh, and here are some grapes leftover from my lunch. You can have them.' So the situation is—someone gives your dad a delicious steak, and someone gives him some leftover grapes. One treat is probably more pleasing. But the other thing is, what if the person who gave the leftover grapes got really mad that his treat was not received as well? What if the grape giver shook his fist and said, 'I can't believe you didn't like what I gave you.'"

Miss Bertie shrugged. "I don't know how it went, but whatever happened that day, God was pleased with what Abel had given, and He was not pleased with what Cain had done. And Cain got mad. So God asks the question we all need to ask ourselves sometimes. 'Why are you angry?'

"Sometimes our feelings, our emotions, are so difficult we don't even understand them ourselves. Why are you angry that your mom asked you to clean up your room? Is it because your little brother doesn't have to clean up his? Is it because you were watching a television program you don't want to miss? Is it because your friends are outside playing, and you want to join them? What is it that is making you angry?

"God asks Cain this question in the Bible, and it's an important one that we need to keep with us. Because if we don't know the answer, we might make a huge mistake. Unfortunately, Cain didn't pay attention to the question and listened instead to his anger. Does anybody know what happens next?"

"Cain … slew … Abel?" Emily asked. She'd heard

these words before and was trying to repeat them just right.

"Indeed he did, and that was a terrible, terrible thing to do. When Cain responded to his anger instead of to God's question, he dishonored what God was trying to teach him, and he decided instead to do a really bad thing.

"Now. What should we do when we know we have done wrong? We might not face a situation as bad as the one Cain and Abel faced. We might be nicer to each other than that. But any of us can get mad at a brother or sister or friend or even parent and stomp off in anger. Any of us can say the wrong thing when we get asked about it.

"So, God asks Cain another question. The first, remember, was, 'Why are you angry?' The second question was, 'Where is your brother?' It's clear that God knows what has happened, and He is giving Cain a chance to confess.

"Now, 'confess' is an adult-like term that helps you make things right after you've done something wrong. The first step in making things right is to admit we have done something wrong. You can almost imagine that after Cain did this terrible thing, if he'd been sitting on the ground weeping over what he had done, God would have had a way to reach his heart and lovingly talk to him about the harm he had caused. But that's not what Cain did. Instead, when God asked Cain where Abel was, Cain gave a response that is almost as famous as 'In the beginning.' He said, 'I know not. Am I my brother's keeper?'

Miss Bertie looked to the row of children. "Dearies, from the beginning of the world, Cain has been an example of how not to do things. He will face the consequences of his attitudes and his actions. From here on out, Cain will wander the earth, and he will no longer enjoy the gifts of farming that the land once provided."

Miss Bertie pushed back a strand of hair as she said, "Cain's in a tough place. Everyone on the earth knows who he is, and they're about to find out what he's done. As this word from God comes to him, he expresses fear for his life—for surely others will want to get back at him for what he did to Abel. But God tells Cain that will not happen. Even in the face of this terrible thing Cain has done, God tells him, 'You are still mine.' God places a mark on him called the Mark of Cain so that others will know not to cause him harm. In doing so, God shows mercy, spares Cain's life, and gives him a chance to think about what he has done wrong.

"In the world of children and parents, this would be like a kid being sent to his room and put in an adult version of time-out. This is a separation that allows the heart to move away from the question a parent may ask us in anger, 'What did you do?' And it moves toward the question that we may feel with sorrow in our hearts, 'What have I done?'

"Children," Miss Bertie concluded, "some of us think about what we have done for a long, long time."

The words from this lesson had barely settled into the room when Mark Daniel poked his head through the door and in a radio-guy mock whisper called to his daughter, "Pssst, Emily. Let's go."

Emily turned to see her dad, then stood up to leave the classroom. As he grabbed her hand in the doorway, she asked more with curiosity than accusation, "Are you angry, Daddy?"

"Not at all, sweetie. Not at all," Mark said. "I just want to make sure we have a good seat in the service."

CHAPTER 7

The Panhandler from the Panhandle

Later that afternoon, Hannah Hayes was cleaning the kitchen for her resting mom as "The Voice of the Family" played in the background. "Well, folks, it's good to be back with you again this afternoon," she heard Mark Daniel say as he began his broadcast. "We had a really special experience in worship and Bible study this a.m. Hope you did as well. Sunday's a time for getting your heart right and your mind straight for heading into the week. And the topic I'd like to focus on today is responsibility. Are we failing our kids if we don't teach them how to become responsible adults? Are we failing society if we don't hold people accountable?

"I mentioned my mom last week, about how she taught me to tie my shoes when I was a kid because she couldn't keep doing this herself. As some of you know, my dad died in a car accident when I was eight years old. I had to become responsible early in life, and let me tell you, I'm not interested in any 'mamby pamby wah wah wah' about how life is hard. Yes, it's hard, and every day is an opportunity to grow up and take responsibility. I had to do it. Everybody has to do it, or society's going to be in a shambles in a hurry. So that's it, folks, today we're talking about responsibility. The phone lines are open."

The calls came in quickly about the state of the world, the problem with the kids these days, the lack of integrity and morality in politicians, and the need to turn back to God.

"So, what's in our way?" Mark Daniel interjected. "If

we know all these things, what's stopping us as a country from turning back to God and living the way we're supposed to live? How can we find our way again, or I should say God's way, am I right? I've got another caller. How's it going today, Eric? Tell us your story."

"Yeah, um, so I listened to your show last week, and this fits with something one of your callers talked about, the one who was at the Piggly Wiggly. But it's really also something of a confession."

"Confession is good for the soul, Eric, so let's hear what you've got to say."

"Okay, so I was a kid here. I grew up in Wellton, but I'd been moving from town to town, doing odd jobs whenever I could get them. So I was down in the Panhandle cleaning up after some storms had come through, and I hadn't been home in a while—about 10 years actually. One day I'd just basically stomped out of the house, told my dad I wasn't coming back. I'd just been kind of wandering around ever since, not really even knowing how to come back."

"Ah, we have a prodigal son, I see," Mark interjected. "That's a tale that's been told many times in many lives. How'd you come back home?"

"Somehow it just worked out that a man was headed this way, and he gave me a ride back to Wellton. My dad didn't know I was here, didn't know I was coming. But anyway, how this connects to the story I heard last week is that this driver had dropped me off in the Piggly Wiggly parking lot, and I was just standing there with my duffel bag trying to figure out what to do next. This might sound weird, but I was going back and forth in my head about Dad's reaction. First, I was already mad that he wasn't going to be happy to see me, but I also really hoped he'd be glad I was there and let me in. I just didn't know what the reality was going to be. I didn't know what was really going to happen when I was at the front door.

"Well, right then, this car comes swerving into the lot and bumps the curb as it pulls into a parking place. It was one of those big, long cars, and the driver's head was about even with the steering wheel. So this kind of interrupted the debate I was having in my head, and I just stood there and watched as the driver's door opens slowly, and this fairly large lady puts her foot on the pavement, then uses the door to pull herself out. So I say, 'Afternoon, ma'am.' Because really, no matter what I've been through, I still try to remember my manners. Then by instinct, it just came out. I asked, 'Ma'am, can you spare a couple of dollars so I can get something to eat?' I mean, that's what I'd done for ten years so it was kind of ingrained in me, I guess."

"Yeah, habits can be quite strong, can't they?" Mark said.

"Sure can, but I was in for a surprise this time. Because let me tell you, that lady looked straight into my face, and dadgum if it wasn't Miss Bertie, my old Sunday school teacher. I knew I was in for it. Frankly, I'd rather be facing a pat-down by the local police. I would have run right then if I could've, but she had me locked in a stare that I could see even through those smudged glasses she was wearing. So she says, 'Eric, what in the Sam Hill are you doing panhandling in the Piggly Wiggly parking lot?'"

Eric gave an uncomfortable laugh as he continued. "Man, I was stumbling out words right and left. 'I'm just, I'm just … I'm just trying to get to my dad's house, Miss Bertie. I was going to pay you back. Honest.'

"'Honest?' she asked. 'I think you better open your dictionary and check the meaning of that word again.'

She had me there, and I'm saying, 'I know, Miss Bertie. I know. I just make it up as I go. I know I do that.' Then we go on to talk about my plan to go home and how I don't even know if Dad's going to let me inside the house. So she tells me when I get to that doorbell, to make sure these two words are stuck in my head and are the only things that are going to come out: 'I'm sorry.' Then I was supposed to say two more words: 'Forgive me.' Miss Bertie told me, 'Take it two words at a time, and you'll find your way back home.' So that's what I did. That's exactly what I did."

"Well, okay then," Mark Daniel said crisply.

"I'll just say to conclude, Dad let me come back home, and I have Miss Bertie to thank for this. She's a good woman." Eric laughed as he added, "She is not slowing down either. I asked her, 'You still teaching that Sunday school class?' She said, 'Eric, I'm going to be teaching that class till they carry me out. And big as I am, carrying me out is not going to be easy to do.'"

"Alrighty," Mark said, "Thanks for your call. Let's see if there's time for one more."

As the program continued, Hannah placed a last dish in the cabinet, then reached to turn off the radio. "I really do need to go see Miss Bertie while I'm here," she said to herself.

CHAPTER 8
The Secret's in the Source

The next afternoon, while reviewing the day's mail in her cubicle at *The Wellton Courier*, Hannah opened an envelope with a return address for The Eternal Rock Community Church. The press release inside announced the purchase of an abandoned structure on the outskirts of town and the intention of reaching a new audience for Christ through worship experiences involving modern music and casual dress.

"Interesting," Hannah said, as someone who might have an opinion on a thing like this came quickly to mind.

Hannah stood to take the short walk to the editor's office. Paul Hill, a crusty, irreligious sort, didn't cotton as well to community mores as perhaps a locally grown editor might have done. When it came to the way the town was doing things, he didn't know not to ask why.

"Paul, I have a press release on a new church … they're taking an interesting approach by having a rock band, and you can wear what you want."

"Yeah?" he asked, as in shorthand for "What's your point?"

"I'd like to go talk to someone local about this—about what this means for churches."

"You going to go talk to the pastor of the Baptist church?" Paul asked.

"No."

"The pastor of the Methodist church?"

"No."

"The head of the deacon body or board of elders or what have you?"

"Well, no ... not yet, I mean."

"Who exactly are you going to talk to?"

"There's this really old first-grade Sunday school teacher I know," Hannah explained. "I'd like to start with her. If that's okay with you."

Paul turned his head to the side for a moment of processing. Then he waved his hand in a "whatever, get-out-of-here" way.

Hannah grabbed her purse and a notebook and headed for the parking lot. Instead of turning the car toward Miss Bertie's home, however, all the food deliveries to her mom gave her the idea to stop by the Piggly Wiggly bakery first to get a treat for her source. It seemed to Hannah that it would be easier to enter a home uninvited when bringing cookies. This technique would give her just a few minutes of transition before she asked, "Did you hear what that new church is doing?"

This is why, moments later, Hannah stepped through the grocery store doors and heard a voice behind her call her name. She twisted around to see a man in a green uniform. "Mitchell?" she responded. "Well, hey. What are you up to these days?"

"Actually I'm just picking up a paycheck, my last one from here. I bagged groceries on the side for the last few years, but I'll be starting a new job soon and don't need the side work anymore."

Mitchell nodded to Hannah. "So. What are you doing now?"

"At the moment I'm picking up some cookies," she answered. "I was going to stop by and see Miss Bertie this afternoon and didn't want to go empty-handed. Remember her?"

"Sure do. She's actually part of the reason I'm changing jobs."

"Really?" Hannah asked, surprised.

"Yeah, she was real motivating when I would take her groceries to the car. She talks a lot, but it's usually good stuff."

"Interesting," Hannah said. The two former classmates quickly concluded their conversation, and she moved toward the bakery section. Approaching the counter, she glanced at the display and asked, "May I get some cookies. Um, let's see, two each of chocolate chip, oatmeal, and sugar?"

"Will that be all?" asked Barbara Johnson as she grabbed the tongs to lift out the cookies.

"Yeah, that's it. A half-dozen cookies."

"Sounds like a nice afternoon snack for you and your mom." Barbara placed the cookies in a sack in this town where most people knew most people. "Little as you are, you can eat what you want anyway," she added, sizing up her customer's fairly small frame.

"Oh, these aren't for us," Hannah explained. "I'm taking them to a lady in my neighborhood—Miss Bertie."

"Miss Bertie? She's a regular. Good person. One time she told me I was doing the Lord's work in the bakery, and I never forgot it."

"Really?" Hannah asked.

"Yeah, she had just picked up several loaves of French bread when I happened to look her way. You make eye contact with her, and the conversation gets going. That's how it is. So she told me she was making a batch of spaghetti for her friends at the halfway house over on Milton Street. Not that I'd asked, but sometimes people just tell you what they're doing. When she rolled her cart closer, she saw that I had a new cake in the display case—

a white-icing sheet cake with some colorful floral designs. 'Lovely, my dear,' she said. 'That's just lovely. You do such fine work.'

"So I told her thanks, that I hope people liked what I did, that I did try to do my best. That's when she starts telling me a Bible story. It seems there was this prophet Elijah who had done these mighty works for the Lord but had this moment where he ran away in fear. Then when Elijah was at his most hopeless, an angel of the Lord came to him and made him a small cake. Miss Bertie said, 'Sometimes, dearie, what we need most in this world is a little piece of cake, and when you are providing the cakes people need to rejuvenate their spirits, you are doing the Lord's work.' Then she paused for a minute, like she was thinking it through, and said, 'I believe I'll take that cake to my friends.'"

"How about that?" Hannah said as Barbara folded the top of the sack over the cookies. "I guess she teaches Sunday school wherever she goes."

"Yeah, I guess so. It really made me think about things." Barbara handed the sack to Hannah. "Oh, and because it's for Miss Bertie, I put in a couple of extra cookies. She might like the white chocolate macadamia we're making now."

"Thanks," Hannah said. "I'm sure she will."

At the time, these two encounters seemed like an extraordinary coincidence. But the thoughts that percolated were ready and waiting when Hannah needed them.

CHAPTER 9

Getting to the Heart of the Matter

Miss Bertie's house on Southview was a short drive away. Hannah pulled into the driveway, grabbed her cookies, purse, and notebook, then stepped out of the car. As she did, she faced a moment of choice: should she go to the front door or the back?

In childhood, she would have been walking through backyards to get here, but now that she was a professional, she headed for the front porch, brushed off a cobweb on the doorbell, and pressed the button. The wait was long enough for Hannah to have second thoughts about her choice. When the front door finally opened, Miss Bertie blinked in the sunlight. "Well, my goodness gracious. Hannah Hayes, what a surprise to see you. Come in this house this instant."

"Hi, Miss Bertie, I brought you cookies for an afternoon treat," Hannah said, holding up the sack as evidence.

"You are a treat yourself, you are so sweet. Come, let us share an afternoon respite together."

"Yes, ma'am," Hannah said as she followed Miss Bertie through the house and entered a small kitchen with a round Formica table accompanied by four metal chairs with yellow cushions in the seat and at the back. The aroma of tasty food preparation was evident. "Smells good in here."

"That's my casserole for tomorrow's meeting of the Wellton Literary Society—poppyseed chicken. I just pulled it out of the oven."

"One of my favorites."

"Join us for the meeting, and I'll serve you up a plate. We convene at ten at the library."

"Oh, I'm afraid I'll be at work, but thank you."

"Please sit and tell me what's new," Miss Bertie said. "May I get you something to sip on while we visit?"

"A little water would be nice."

The elderly lady lifted a glass out of the cabinet as Hannah asked, "Miss Bertie, did you hear that a new congregation, The Eternal Rock Community Church, bought the empty building out on Piedmont?"

"That old distribution warehouse?"

"Yes, ma'am."

"Well, why do suppose they did that? What kind of packing and shipping will they be doing?" Miss Bertie turned on the faucet, and water flowed into the glass.

Hannah shrugged. "I guess the people kind. It's a different kind of church. They're going to set up an auditorium, have a rock band. You can wear whatever you want. But it's not just for Sundays. They'll have services on Friday nights, and they'll have these large screens where you can watch the band and watch the preacher."

"Isn't that interesting?" Miss Bertie said as she opened a freezer door to grab a couple of chunks of ice. She dropped them into the water and set the glass in front of Hannah.

"Yeah, and as I understand how these things work—they won't have hymnbooks and Bibles in the pews. The lyrics and scripture will be on the screens."

"Well, my goodness," Miss Bertie said. "Imagine that." She shook her head in amazement as she continued, "I tell you, I sure have seen a lot in my time. So many changes. I had just come into the world and said howdy the same year Wilbur and Orville Wright opened the first civilian flying school on farmland in Montgomery. It didn't last. But I think of that because there was a bicycle repairman who lived pretty far out on Earlie Street. He's not the kind of man that I would have looked at and said, 'He's the kind of man who would have invented an airplane.' Instead, I would have said, 'That's the man who repairs bicycles.'"

Miss Bertie pulled out a chair and joined Hannah at the table. "So what I'm saying is, you don't always see who people truly are, or what they could become—that's for sure. But what really matters is what they're willing to see within themselves. If I were to pick a person to be an aviation pioneer, I probably would have picked someone with an engineering degree instead of two brothers who repaired bicycles, among other things, and didn't complete high school."

"I guess you're right, Miss Bertie."

"Yes, and this is just another reason we should all be glad that I am not in charge of the world. If you hear their names now—the Wright Brothers—you will associate them with their pivotal moment in aviation history. They were also ordinary men who looked at the sky and asked, 'Why not?' Well, we've all seen the sky, but most of us don't ask, 'Why not?' So, getting back to the topic at hand, perhaps that's what that new church is doing. Somebody sat in a committee and asked, 'Why not?'"

Miss Bertie peered into the sack. "These look delicious. Let's dig in, shall we?" She retrieved a couple of cookies and placed them on napkins for her and her guest.

Hannah pulled one of the cookies closer as she continued her interview. "Well, Miss Bertie, what about watching a worship service on a large screen? Does that seem like a good kind of church experience?"

Miss Bertie shrugged. "I suppose a screen can be useful. I couldn't say. It really matters more what you do with what you hear. Is there something superior to someone not doing the work of the Lord after hearing about it in a sanctuary than if someone doesn't do the work of the Lord after hearing about it in a distribution center? Or vice versa, clearly."

Hannah nodded. "Good point."

Miss Bertie switched subjects. "So, tell me, dearie, how's your mom doing?"

"She's okay, I guess. The chemo has zapped her energy, as it does. She's home resting."

Miss Bertie mused, "For so much of our lives our mothers seem like the center of the universe, the person we cling to and push and pull against until we become who we are. It's hard to see our mothers face illness."

"Yes, ma'am."

"And so soon after your dad's accident. I know this is a tough time for your family. I will be praying for you, that you will be stronger than you ever knew you could be."

"Thank you, Miss Bertie," Hannah said as her voice cracked. "I just didn't see things going this way. Daddy's accident was hard on all of us. Then things went south with this guy I was dating. Now with Mom's illness, I moved back home. I don't like to think about what's ahead, so I keep that door closed."

"Yes, those doors … it's hard to know when to open them and welcome who you're becoming, or when to close them and let go of who you were. There's an expression you may have heard—Go out the way you came in—that has to do with leaving a house by the same door you entered or else you'll be unlucky. Have you heard it?"

"No, I'm not familiar with that one."

"In a sense, I'm taking this saying to heart. I started my earthly life in this very house in 1910. Lord willing, this is where I'll return to my eternal home. Yet there were a lot of doors in the meantime. I had to make a lot of choices."

"So what did you do? How did you proceed?" Hannah asked, curious what else her old teacher might offer.

"I just did the thing in front of me, dearie. It turns out that life is lived in increments … five minutes, fifteen minutes, thirty minutes. Basically, this moment, that moment. And moment by moment, you go through your day taking care of the things in front of you."

Miss Bertie took a sip of water before continuing. "So, dearie, what is the thing in front of you? What brings you out on a lovely afternoon with cookies and questions?"

"Well," Hannah said as she shifted from her new-church-in-town questions to something that all of a sudden held a great deal more interest. "I'd like to hear more about your story, Miss Bertie. I'd like to know more about your choices, your doors."

"My dear, that is a long story indeed."

"I'm really interested. I'd like to hear it," Hannah pressed.

"Well, let me see … how shall I present myself in the right context? We probably don't have time to go back to the beginning of the world, but what if we start in this house?"

"Please begin."

CHAPTER 10

Miss Bertie Dusts Off
an Old Story

"Trash day is tomorrow, and I've started to think of this experience almost as an act of communion," Miss Bertie began. "It's a time of releasing. I have this idea that whenever I throw something away, I'm doing the future a favor. By that, I'm saying those little children who come to clean out this house when I'm gone will appreciate everything they don't have to remove.

"Oh, they won't be little children then, obviously—this will be my older brothers' grandchildren. They'll be grown and have so much in their own homes that they'll probably just get the good stuff and set the other things on the curb for Thursday trash pickup. Fine by me. The older I get, the less this stuff matters.

"Still, I need something to sit on every day until I'm gone, and I wouldn't mind watching a little television. But I can't put my own chair on the curb and dispose of my own electronics. For this, you need family.

"Here's the problem. How will they know? What if they think the treasures are the big pieces, the functional things? Or what if they hold onto things I held onto because they don't know what to do with them?"

Miss Bertie took a sip of water as she searched for her point. "Let's say they find a grocery store receipt from twenty-five years ago," she continued. "Will they wonder why I saved it? Will they be mesmerized by the price of flour in 1970, or will they sense, instinctively, 'She wasn't a very good housekeeper?' If I clean things out, no one has to ask those questions."

Hannah nodded. "That makes sense. When my dad died, I came across a list of things he'd meant to pick up at the hardware store—outdoor faucet covers, new air conditioning filter, stuff like that. This was in his car, and I was confused. I didn't know if finding the list was a reminder that details like these aren't important, or if this was a sign that I could honor his memory by taking care of details like these. I had no idea. Still don't, really."

"I'm sorry, dear," Miss Bertie said, acknowledging the poignancy of the comment. "And someone will walk around my kitchen and ask the same kind of questions as they come across strips of slightly used aluminum foil or the plastic bags I've saved from loaves of bread. Is it just stuff? Or does it represent a lasting message about my life?" Miss Bertie shrugged.

"Mom has a drawer with stuff like that," Hannah said, offering a slight nod.

Miss Bertie smiled as she added, "Also, there's a good bit of dust in here. I left it on the furniture so it'd be easy to find."

"So far this sounds a lot like our house," Hannah said, returning the smile.

"There are some other things here as well. I'm leaving behind a treasure trove of teachers' gifts. You can probably spot those because they're small. Small trinkets, small books, small figurines—basically small things that sit around a house. Then there are the really large pieces of furniture—pieces Papa made or purchased when the home was new. They'll call these antiques, and they are, but at one time they were just beds and tables."

Miss Bertie paused, as if a different thought had taken center stage. She leaned her large frame on the table to steady her rise from the chair. "My dear, there is something else in this house that you might be interested in. Or maybe I presume too much, and the truth is, this is what I am interested in, and I'm going to compel your interest." Miss Bertie winked. "A teacher's prerogative, wouldn't you say?"

"I'm interested already," Hannah replied. She rose and followed her teacher into the musty coolness of a darkened dining room as Miss Bertie flipped on the light switch.

"There's a lesson in here ... a big one ... in the buffet against the wall."

"Nice piece," Hannah said.

"I'm sure by many measures it is. Mahogany and all that. But more importantly, if you'll look in the drawer on the right, you'll see that it is divided in slots. The third slot has a pile of linen napkins. Beneath those napkins is a plastic bag, and in that plastic bag is a frail and aging letter. That's what I'd like for you to see."

Crossing the room in front of her host, Hannah reached to pull the drawer and, in doing so, shook a cloud of dust from its resting place.

"Third slot?" Hannah confirmed.

"Yes, under the napkins."

As Hannah lifted out the plastic bag, Miss Bertie explained, "This is a letter my grandfather wrote home from a Civil War camp way back in 1862. Inside, the paper is as sturdy as a biscuit flake. To touch it, open it, is to risk disintegration. After so much time, the pencil marks are fading. Yet the embers of these words still smolder. I can almost smell the burning, as if I were walking through that desolate land myself. Though mostly I feel it."

Miss Bertie held up a finger of caution. "Let me hasten to add, there's nothing to idealize about that experience— not about the immorality at the heart of the conflict or the devastation endured by the men fighting to preserve an immoral way of life. When history becomes just a set of words, you don't realize the suffering that reached into so many lives. It was definitely there, however, and still seeps into who we became."

"May I read it?" Hannah asked, holding the envelope gingerly.

"Yes, by all means. Let's reposition ourselves at the dining room table and continue our chat." They pulled out a pair of heavy chairs as Miss Bertie wiped dust off the table with her sleeve. "My apologies. I haven't been in here in a while." Hannah carefully lifted the letter out of the envelope and unfolded the fragile paper.

"I have seen nothing of what my grandfather saw," Miss Bertie continued. "Even so, that sense of calamity, of being hard pressed, of wondering how things would end, and if you'd ever see family again ... that rings true. There is no temptation that is not common to man, the scriptures tell us. I wasn't in my grandfather's battle. Still, the feelings ring true—at least for me. Read it and you'll see what I mean."

CHAPTER 11

A Homesick Soldier's Letter Home

Hannah struggled through the old-style handwriting composed in faded pencil marks but managed to make it through to the end as the experience of one soldier from long ago came back to life in her hands:

Tupelo, Mississippi
June 11th, 1862

Dear Mother and Sisters,

I arose this morning with the sun as before in undespairing, able health and thank God for His blessings and trusting to God that this may find you all enjoying the same blessings. Mother and Sisters, months and years have passed over my head since I have seen either of you and I have once thought that I would never see you again on earth, but I now live in hopes that I will see you all again, but if I never should meet either of you on earth again, I hope to meet you all in Heaven, if it should be God's will.

Mother and Sisters, the enemy crowded around us so at Corinth, Mississippi, with such heavy force that we had to leave the place and march by land quick time about seventy-five miles where we are now in camp at Tupelo. A great many of our soldiers gave out on the way and were picked up by the enemy. We burned all of our tents and beds and wearing clothes only what we could carry on our backs. We suffered a great deal for water, and the dust was very bad. We destroyed everything in our country as we marched, burned everything in the line of provisions, cotton and all kinds of stock etc., that we could not drive before us. In short, the country was burning as we marched through.

There is no use to describe the army to you for I know you have heard all about it. It is impossible for this army to be whipped if it is properly managed, but bad management and neglect will do most anything. Mother and Sisters, we have sixty or sixty-five thousand sick soldiers here in this army, and we must now have somewhere near two-hundred-thousand fighting men now on the fields. As for our camp and army we have lost some by sickness, some have fell in the battle field, some wounded and some taken prisoners. In short, our company has suffered a great deal here in Mississippi.

Mother and Sisters, I have seen the bomb shells and cannon balls come whistling through the air at me, and I have heard the musket balls whistle by my ears but none have touched my body. In short, I have been in places that I thought every moment that a ball would hit me but I am yet unhurt, and no doubt the Yankees have felt the power of my balls that I shot at them.

I could write to you all day and then not tell you one half of my sorrows, trials and troubles here in camps, but I hope I will live to see you all then and we can talk it all over.

I want you all to write to me regular and not wait for me to write you for my chances are bad. I received several letters from some of you when I was sick at Mobile that I never did get to read. I was too sick and they were put in my trunk, and clothes and all were burned at Corinth, Mississippi, on our retreat from that place.

Mother and Sisters, I want you all to pray for me that I may live to fight through the battles and come out untouched and return to my family. And Mother, if I should fall in the course, I want you to remember my daughter for she feels dear to me as a lovely daughter. My wife is teaching school at Wessobulga and my daughter is going to school. You all must write to her at Wessobulga. I must close with tears in my eyes. Give my love to all.

Your son and brother in war,

Manuel

"My goodness, the letter really gives you a sense of the experience," Hannah said when she reached the close. "Did your grandfather make it home? Did he return to his wife and daughter?"

"That answer is complicated," Miss Bertie said. "Yet it is a point of departure for everything that came later, including me. I'll tell you more about all of that another time. It seems I've talked and talked, my dear, and could use a little sustenance. May I fix you a bite to eat for supper? I'm sure I have something around here I can rustle up. I'm sorry that the poppyseed chicken will have to wait till tomorrow, but perhaps some chicken salad?"

"Oh, thank you, but no, ma'am. I need to go check on my mother," Hannah said. "She has a lot of food anyway from friends who keep bringing dishes." Hannah gingerly returned the flimsy paper to the flimsy envelope, then placed the letter back in the plastic bag. "Shall I put this back in the drawer under the linen napkins?"

"Yes, please."

As Hannah moved from her chair back to the buffet, she said, "I would really like to learn more, Miss Bertie. I'd like to hear about what came later. May I come visit again?"

"Certainly, my dear. You are welcome anytime."

CHAPTER 12

The Germ of an Idea

Moments later, as Hannah walked toward her car in the driveway, Myra Hamilton's Buick Park Avenue was heading down Southview. The large sedan slowed and came to a stop across the street. The older lady waved an arm and yelled out of the window, "Hannah, dear, so nice to see you back in town."

"It's good to be here." Hannah stepped to the edge of the driveway to greet the driver.

"Sure do miss your dad."

Hannah nodded. "Me too." Hannah's dad Martin had been director of marketing for Hamilton Sock Company for many years and had worked with Myra's husband, Tom.

"How's Miss Bertie doing?"

"Seems to be doing well," Hannah said as she heard the sound of a car turn the corner. "Um, Mrs. Hamilton, there's someone coming up behind you."

"Call me, Myra, dear, and they'll go around." Myra lifted her hand in the air to motion to the other driver to do just that. As a young man pulled around, he slowed his car between Myra and Hannah, shaking his head as if to indicate his displeasure.

"You have a nice visit with Miss Bertie?" Myra continued.

"I did indeed. She and I go way back."

Myra raised her voice to be heard over the roadway. "Such a lovely lady, but I'm actually upset right now about what they're trying to do to her. I shouldn't say anything, but it's just not right."

"Who's trying to do something to Miss Bertie?" Hannah asked, concerned. She stepped into the road to move closer to the driver's window as another car approached. Hannah lifted her hand to wave it around.

"Truly, I shouldn't even bring it up, but it's really been on my heart. I just get the sense that some people think Miss Bertie is too old to teach children about God. They brought it up in a meeting, for heaven's sake. That young man on the radio did. The one that does the call-in show."

"Mark Daniel?" Hannah asked with surprise.

"Yes, that's the one." Myra paused and shook her head. "Now people have just started talking about it, like it's a thing we need to deal with. I know I shouldn't say anything, but, like I said, it's really been on my heart. And I bet it would never have even come up if that new church wasn't opening up."

"So, word is out about Eternal Rock?" Hannah asked.

"Oh, indeed. Right here in Wellton. Can you imagine? All so some people who don't want to wear ties and dresses can listen to a concert instead of singing the Gospel from our hymn books." Myra shook her head again. "Times sure are changing, Hannah."

"Yes, they are."

Myra nodded her head toward Miss Bertie's house. "All I know is, that's a faithful woman in there. Never misses a Sunday, and who am I going to put in her place if they take her out?" Then she shifted subjects. "Well, I best be getting home. Tom will want his supper soon. Good to see you, Hannah. Tell your sweet momma I said hey."

"I will."

With a short drive around the corner, Hannah pulled into her own driveway and moved quickly up the front steps. Entering through the living room and moving into the kitchen, she assessed her surroundings. There was a saucepan in the sink and a little remaining liquid in the coffee maker on the counter which sat next to a box overstuffed with recipe cards. She could hear the hum of the refrigerator. Turning, she also noted a new aluminum foil-wrapped delivery sitting on the stovetop. Hannah peeked in to discover a freshly made loaf of bread, still slightly warm.

Just past the screen door to the backyard, Hannah heard birds singing here and there and a dog's bark in the distance. She moved down the hallway toward the sounds of a TV anchorman where she found her mother sitting in an armchair in the master bedroom, engaged in a newspaper crossword puzzle and taking in news of the day from a small television set on the dresser.

"Hello, sweetie," her mother said. "Why don't I fix us a bite to eat? We just have so much food from everyone stopping by."

"You seem to be feeling better," Hannah said.

"Oh, I am doing quite well today. I've gotten a lot of my energy back since that last round of chemo. I'm doing quite well indeed. Even had a chance to mop the floor this afternoon—believe me, it needed mopping."

Hannah felt gratitude for the optimism that seemed to come so naturally to her mother, even if she wasn't entirely sure the optimism was warranted. They ate a quick supper, cleaned up the dishes, then Hannah retreated to her bedroom where she powered up her computer. For a long, silent moment, she stared at the empty screen as she looked for words of wisdom from her own life. And came up with nothing.

Standing, she reached into a drawer for her pajamas, then walked into the hallway bathroom where she grabbed a toothbrush on the counter. As the water from the faucet ran into the sink, Hannah stared in the mirror, noting changes in a familiar face. Fair skin, round face, blue eyes, a few fading freckles on the nose, surrounded by light brown hair—they showed a mix of both mother and father in one image. But where was she in this picture?

Martin Hayes returned to her memory. The weekend after his mother's funeral, three years ago by now, she'd found her father in the living room with his head in his hands quietly weeping. He and her Aunt Frieda had spent the day in her grandmother's apartment dividing furniture and belongings, and Martin had gotten a box of his own baby pictures. He wiped his eyes with his handkerchief and returned it to his pocket. "When you become the caretaker of your own baby pictures," he explained to Hannah, "that's a very sad day."

That afternoon he'd showed her images of a little boy who'd had big dreams of flying in space ships to the moon. But when his adulthood came, he'd mostly been a dad in a small town, going to work at a company day in and day out.

"It's been good, though," he said with sincerity. "When you're a kid, you don't realize how good the ordinary can be. You end up going through life doing the things you need to do, and somehow the stuff of dreams becomes the place you lay your head down each night." Martin returned the photos to the box as he added as if only for himself, "Even on a day like this, it's been pretty good."

From that not-so-distant time and space, Hannah could almost hear her father say, "Don't worry about us. Do what you're here to do. Keep your eyes open and find your story." From those thoughts, sentences began to emerge. Hannah dropped her toothbrush in the holder and returned to her computer, where she typed:

Miss Bertie is so old, she could have been Methuselah's big sister. But that doesn't mean she doesn't have a lesson or two for the kids these days.

In doing so, she'd possibly found the one thing she could actually write about: someone else. Hannah would file a quick story on the new church for the paper, yet she would also make plans to learn more about her elderly teacher.

She checked the time—7 p.m.—and decided to roll the dice on the first call. She reached for the phone book sitting under her bedroom's princess-style extension and scanned the letter J for Jackson. There were quite a few listings for the common surname, but she quickly narrowed down Mitchell's number, picked up the receiver, and began to dial.

CHAPTER 13
The Son Rises at Dawn

The next afternoon at the drug store on Earlie Street, *The Wellton Courier's* ace reporter situated herself at a table near the soda fountain. Moments later, she watched as the man in a green uniform pushed open the door, gave her a nod, and headed in her direction.

"Thank you for coming," she said.

"Sure," he replied as he pulled out a chair. "I'm sorry I haven't had a chance to get cleaned up. I just got off work."

"Do you mind if I record this conversation?" she asked. "It will help me with my notes."

"That's fine. Whatever."

Placing a mini-cassette recorder on the table, Hannah asked, "And your name is …"

"You serious? You know my name, Hannah. We grew up together. You called me last night."

"Yes, but I'm a reporter now, and I'm just trying to make it official. Like, in case you decide to sue me later for a spelling mishap."

"Mitchell, alright? My name is Mitchell Jackson. M-i-t-c-h-e-l-l J-a-c-k-son. So, you still Hayes?"

"Yes, still Hannah Hayes. And your age?"

He shrugged. "Well, just like you I guess, I'm thirty years old."

"Okay," Hannah said. "If you would, please tell me in your own words a little about yourself. What you do, where you've been working, and then we'll get to what happened at the Piggly Wiggly."

"I've been working at the elementary school. I'm on the custodial staff."

"What's your day like there?"

"Pretty basic stuff, really. Each morning at 6:00 a.m., I pour red granules on the tile floor and sweep the school hallway."

Mitchell relaxed as he settled into his description. "The smell of that stuff tickles my nose. Old Mr. Burns had told me I'd never get that smell out of my memory, and he was right. He's the one who had the job before me."

"Yes, I remember him. So, how do things go with the kids in the school?"

"How do they 'go'? About like you'd expect, I guess. The kids start coming in around 7:15. It's like they can't even see me, but I'm not invisible. They see their friends and enemies, the places they want to sit, the groups they want to join, the people they want to please. They're not thinking about any school janitor but about whatever angle they're working. You know, I was like that too once upon a time—a kid with dreams about the world. But there was also this thing inside me that laughed at all that and told me I wasn't worth it. That's why that stuff at the Piggly Wiggly mattered so much."

A waitress stopped by the table and asked, "Y'all need anything?"

"Lime-aid," they both said. This was a sweet concoction like lemonade but with limes.

"Alright," the waitress said. "Be right back."

Mitchell continued, "I was telling Miss Bertie that I always had to go straight home after work because those red granules stick to me, and I need to change out of my uniform. I didn't want to smell like a janitor out in the world. I don't remember exactly how she said it, but she explained that the real problem isn't when something sticks on your clothes but when something sticks inside your spirit, and you take that out in the world."

"This was at the Piggly Wiggly that she said this?"

"Yeah, I'd see her there sometimes. I'd gotten a side job bagging groceries on the weekends. Anyway, there was this one time when I was carrying her groceries to the car, and she asked me if I'd ever thought about going to the community college. I told her I wasn't cut out for that. 'Be careful what you let stick to you, Mitchell,' she said, and it got me started thinking about things."

"And … ?"

"Well, the next time I carried her bags to the car, I started telling her about sweeping the floors at the school and how nothing I was doing mattered. So she said, 'Mitchell, when you're using your hands to make the world a better place—in your case cleaner, with less trash—you're doing work that matters.'

"I told her, 'But it doesn't last, Miss Bertie. I mean, what about when a kid vomits right after I sweep the floor? I make a difference for five minutes?'

"Well, she pointed a crooked, arthritic finger in my face and said, 'Mitchell, in one way or another, people are always throwing up on the work we do. You're no different than anyone else. Even the principal has parents and school board members coming up there trying to throw up on the work he's doing. Figuratively speaking, of course.'

"So I opened the backdoor of her big old car and placed two bags in the seat. I was really thinking about what she said … how everybody, even the owner of the grocery store, had complainers who would come in and throw up on their work. But for them it would come out like, 'This price is a rip-off. Why are you out of the stuff I want? This milk is bad.' Stuff like that. I was starting to get a picture in my head, and I said, 'People spew out a lot of stuff, don't they, Miss Bertie?'

"'They sure do,' she said, 'It's been that way since the beginning of the world.'"

The waitress set two paper cups on the table. "Here you go. Need anything else?"

"That's all, thank you," Hannah answered.

"Alright then," the waitress said. "When you're done, just go up to the cash register and tell them what you had. I'm getting off now."

Mitchell said, "Thanks, Linda Sue. We'll see you next time."

Hannah turned her attention back to her interview. "How did these incidents usually end?"

"About the same, really. She'd fold her large body into the front seat and say, 'Now. Go make a difference somewhere. Good day to you, son.'"

Mitchell took a long drink of his lime-aid. "I've got to tell you. She really made me think about things. I mean, I really did apply to that community college, just like she suggested."

"How'd that go?"

"It started out kind of weird. Looking back, I'd say the longest walk I ever took was from the parking lot to the door of the admissions office. It was like I heard a dozen people yelling 'go/don't go' inside my head. But once inside, things got a lot easier. I'll be getting my associate's degree in business soon."

"What will you do now?"

"I'm about to start a job working in customer service for a lumber plant. I'm going to help organize the customer orders and make sure they're delivered to the right place. If needed, I guess you could say, I'll clean up the vomit when something goes wrong. Figuratively speaking, of course."

The reporter and interviewee spoke and sipped for a few more minutes as Hannah clicked off her recorder and dropped her notebook in her purse.

"So, if that's what you needed, I'm going to head home and get out of this uniform," Mitchell said.

"Sure thing. I'll take care of the bill."

As Mitchell headed out of the door, Hannah approached the register and told the older lady behind the counter, "I'm paying for two lime-aids."

In response, the older lady said, "Hannah, you and Mitchell Jackson seeing each other now?"

Hannah's face flushed. "No, ma'am, Miss Pauline. This is a work thing. I'm a reporter at *The Wellton Courier*. This was an interview."

"Interview?" Miss Pauline said, tilting her head. "Well, that's a dollar sixty-five for the lime-aids." Hannah pulled out two dollar bills as Miss Pauline asked, "So, how's your mom doing? I heard she'd been sick."

"She's doing pretty well, actually. I'll tell her you asked about her."

"You do that. I'm sure she's glad to have you here."

"Thank you, Miss Pauline."

Over the next few weeks, there would be more stories like Mitchell's that Hannah would uncover. But why? What was Miss Bertie's why? She would keep digging.

CHAPTER 14

The Electrician Makes a Connection

Just after lunch the next day, Paul Hill poked his head into Hannah's cubicle. "There's a wreck on Piedmont. Can you go get it?"

It was an order, not a question, but Hannah answered yes, she would go get it.

At the edge of town, she snapped a photo of two cars that collided as one crossed the railroad tracks into the oncoming traffic on Piedmont. She noted that a passenger had an injury and was treated at the scene.

As she scribbled names and details, light drops of rain began to fall on her notepad. She kept writing, but it was just enough of a nudge for the grief within her to swell as the sounds and smells brought reminders of unexpected loss. When the wrecker came to transport one of the vehicles to the Wellton Body Shop, she reentered her car and took the long way back to the newsroom.

You don't think about things early on—what a sidewalk means, or a curve in the road, or a tree, Hannah observed. They are just there, like parents, there, always there. But a sidewalk is not without a street, and a tree is not in its place without wind and rain and other forces of nature. When the large oak at the corner of Southview and Earlie fell one stormy night, the life Hannah had known flipped on its axis.

Hannah swam through these thoughts as she drove along Piedmont, but came back to present day when she noticed a service vehicle for Ford Electrical at the former distribution center. She pulled into the parking lot as a man in work boots bearing a familiar face walked through the drizzle toward his truck.

"Earl?" she called from her car window.

Earl Ford turned toward her voice with a curious look. "Hannah?" he asked as he came closer. "Girl, if it was you that brought this rain to town, we're good, okay? You can get it to stop now."

"I'll see what I can do," she said with a smile. "So, what's going on here?"

"Putting in some wiring for the new church. You can't have a rock band without an electrician, you know."

"You planning to join them for services?"

"You kidding me? Miriam Ford would unleash every prayer in her arsenal if I stepped outside of that Catholic church she helped start. I'm just here to install the wiring and say 'Y'all enjoy.'"

Just then another car pulled into the lot. "Who's this?" Earl asked. "Are you being followed by a secret admirer?"

Hannah shrugged. "Probably somebody turning around."

"No, wait, it's that radio guy," Earl said as the driver lifted a hand in a wave. "What's his name?"

"Mark Daniel?"

"Yeah, what's he doing here?" They watched from a distance as Mark stepped out of his car into the sprinkling drops of rain and began a casual walk around the property.

"Maybe he's out looking for a story, something to talk about on Sunday," Hannah suggested.

"I suppose," Earl said, turning back to Hannah's car window. "You know, when he was a kid, he lost his dad in an accident out this way."

"Really? I guess we have something in common."

"Everybody's got something in common, girl."

Hannah snorted. "You're deeper than you look, Earl."

"I try," Earl said with a wink. "You have a good one."

Earl got in his truck and pulled out of the parking lot as Hannah watched Mark Daniel peer into a window. "What *is* he doing here?" she wondered as she drove away.

CHAPTER 15
A Time of Terrible Days

On Saturday Hannah had a free schedule, and it seemed like a good day for a long visit—assuming Miss Bertie was available. So she stopped by that afternoon. This time she walked around the house where she could see Miss Bertie through the screen door loading a plate into her dishwasher as the radio crackled with music from the public station. Hannah rapped on the frame.

"Oh, Hannah, how delightful to see you this fine day," Miss Bertie said, turning to push the door open.

"I hope you don't mind my dropping by again."

"Not at all, not at all. I had actually been preparing myself to dust the dining room, based on what we saw the other day. You have thankfully interrupted my plans. Please come in this house right this instant and distract me from that noble effort."

Hannah smiled as she stepped through the doorway. "I really did want to hear more of your story."

"Oh, my. Talking is what I do best. It's my spiritual gift, you might say, and I'm always glad to regale you with tales from this old life. May I fix you something to drink? Or would you like a bite to eat?"

"No, ma'am, I don't want you to go to any trouble. I'd just like to visit, if we can."

"My dear, you might as well have asked if I'd like a free trip to Disney World. Let's make our way to the den so we can get comfortable and have a little chat."

Miss Bertie took her seat in a soft but well-worn

armchair as Hannah found her place on an old sofa. She set her purse on the coffee table and pulled out a notebook. "Last time I was here, I'd asked you if your grandfather survived the war, and you said, 'That answer is complicated.' I'd like to hear that complicated answer."

"Happy to oblige," Miss Bertie said.

"Do you mind if I let this recorder run while we talk?" Hannah asked. "I'd like to make some notes, and this will help."

"Well, I'm sure you'll want to shut that off the very moment I start singing, but as long as I'm talking, I'm sure that's fine as well." Hannah leaned toward the end table next to Miss Bertie, pressed record, and set the small device near her interviewee.

"So, your grandfather fought in the Civil War and wrote a letter home that evoked a difficult experience," Hannah said, restating what she'd learned as an interview prompt. "Can you tell me more about his time at war?"

"Oh, what terrible days those must have been," Miss Bertie reflected, leaning back in her chair. "First, I can hardly imagine why he was there, and how all these terrible things had to happen for the men in Montgomery to say, 'Let's start this war.' I'm not sure what Manuel's thinking was on the fear and anger, the sense of threat rising up around him. Did he want to fight for the right to own slaves? I don't know. But I do know he went to war. When a point of view is fomenting around you, people get swept up. They do right in their own eyes, scripture says. So young men went off to fight the battles started by other men to protect the structure that underpinned the economy."

"I have trouble seeing how people saw it as the right thing—that slavery was right," Hannah interjected.

"Yes, even the churches approved, and toxins people

had been fed from birth took hold." Miss Bertie paused to gather her thoughts. "So there was anger, a great deal that rose up. But back to the point, while Manuel was away, he bought a sheet of paper—cost him a nickel of his pay—in order to write a letter home. That's what you read. By that time, he was in misery."

"Yeah, it sounded like a hard time. Do you know more about those days?"

"Well, Manuel obviously had a before and after," she answered her guest. "Before the war, he was a husband and father. He was also a merchant and a Mason, and over time he'd gotten to know a Yankee businessman—a man who sold goods to merchants in the area. They'd met at a Masonic convention over in West Point, Georgia, and had become friends. Then the war came, and Manuel joined in the fight for the Confederacy.

"These war years were difficult, no question about it. Many of the young boys died not from the battles but from dysentery, influenza, and other severe ailments. Manuel came close to that outcome himself. He had many days of illness. He also knew hunger. And things got worse. Just a few months after he wrote that letter, he was wounded during a battle up in Kentucky. The injury was severe but survivable, and in his injured state he was taken to a prisoner of war camp in Cairo, Illinois. What happened next was something strangely charitable for wartime. The POW camp had an open house. This was something that happened early in the war. People from the enemy side could come see the prisoners, render medical assistance and aid, as well as find out who was there and get word back to family.

"That's the other part of the story. That Yankee business associate and fellow Mason heard about the camp in Cairo and attended the open house where he came upon his old buddy. There's no proof but a theory that he somehow intervened. Within days, Manuel was added to a prisoner exchange list, taken by steamer down the Mississippi, and railed on over to Mobile, where he was placed in a hospital to receive the medical attention he desperately needed if he were to survive. This intervention, stroke of luck, or happenstance is the reason I am able to tell you this story. This was almost the endpoint, the eraser of all that came later. But Manuel survived, and for the remainder of his days, he credited the Yankee and the Masons with saving his life."

"Ah. He lived. So he was able to come home after that?" Hannah assumed.

"Not quite," Miss Bertie said. "My existence is not assured just yet."

"I'm still listening."

CHAPTER 16
Trouble That Doesn't End

"Let's put it this way," Miss Bertie explained. "You're probably familiar with people who are unsympathetic. You go through trouble, make some kind of mistake, and they say, 'Well, that's what you get.'

"That's what happened to Manuel, so to speak. He had been Fifth Sergeant of his company prior to getting wounded in battle. After he got shot, captured, exchanged, and returned to his regiment, he was demoted to private. The thinking was like this: 'If you're going to get yourself shot, you must have been doing something wrong. Furthermore, your injury and capture are signs that God's grace is not with you which for certain means you're doing something wrong.' You might call that 'adding insult to injury.'"

"He got demoted for getting shot and captured?" Hannah asked.

"That's what appears to have happened. On the other hand, perhaps Manuel had a personality his commanding officer regarded with suspicion. Manuel might not have operated comfortably within the structure of military service, and his commanding officer may have had the thought, 'This is just like something he would do.' Who knows? I don't. But I do know Manuel survived his hunger, his illness, his injury, his capture, his exchange, and his demotion during this terrible war, and his survival ensured that my existence became possible."

"So he did come back to his wife and daughter," Hannah presumed.

"Not exactly. My fate was not contingent upon the wife teaching at Wessobulga and his dear daughter going to school there, for it was actually in spite of them."

"How so?"

"Well, Manuel served for the full time the Confederacy was at war, returning home after four years away. Unfortunately, that's when he was given by a friend the unwelcome news that his wife had had an affair during his absence. Their marriage was over, and Manuel filed for divorce."

"Oh. I didn't see this plot point coming, actually," Hannah said.

"Indeed," Miss Bertie responded. "Nonetheless, Manuel was here, war weary and rejected and in need of a new start. In the months and years that followed, he arranged for the loan and eventual purchase of forty acres of land in east Alabama not far from Wellton. The property would be adjacent to the land occupied by a widow and her three children. As Manuel worked the field to the south of this property, the two people with holes in their lives from previous marriages became acquainted. Then they became husband and wife. Then they brought into this world two more children, one of whom became my Papa."

"Ah, and this will lead to you."

"Yes, I arrived some years later myself and have been living ever since in the grace of someone else's terrible days. For if friends and countrymen had not taken up arms against each other in a devastating fight over an immoral cause, and if in the meantime Manuel's first wife had not left him for someone else, I would not have been born."

"I guess we don't always realize what took place to get us here … the struggles others lived through that made our own lives possible," Hannah said, shaking her head.

"Very true, yet here I am," Miss Bertie said. "I did pop up at my moment in history, and over time I ventured into my own battlefields, though by my social training, I spoke of my experiences as if I were walking through a garden on a sunny afternoon and all was well."

"What do you mean, Miss Bertie?" Hannah asked, realizing how little she knew about her subject's personal life.

"Oh, these were the days when I couldn't figure it out, couldn't find my way. Sinking, falling, spiraling. You pick the image. Even so, something else was at work. I felt it, sensed it. And as I fell, I whispered to the heavens, 'What do I do?' I heard an answer, one almost too simple to believe. But there it was, this voice speaking through my despair and offering up a fairly basic idea: 'Follow Me.'"

Miss Bertie looked to the clock on the wall. "I'm sorry, my dear, but this would be a good time to take a break. I am an old teacher, you know, and somewhere in my head I hear a school bell ringing. After a certain period, I have a sense that it's time to conclude my lesson."

"Perfectly understandable, Miss Bertie. I'm glad to get these doses of insight in whatever increments you provide them."

"Would you like for me to fix you a pimento cheese sandwich? I made some fresh just this morning. I have a little vegetable soup to go with it."

"Oh no, thank you, Miss Bertie, but I hope you'll let me come back again. Perhaps tomorrow?"

"Indeed I will. I usually go to the Piggly Wiggly on Sunday, but you're more than welcome to stop by later."

"I'll try to do that."

"Will you be joining us at the service in the morning?"

"I'm not sure," Hannah deflected. "I'll probably just stay home with mom. If she feels like getting out, I will, but otherwise, I'll stay with her."

It'd been a long time since Hannah had been to church.

CHAPTER 17

The Talk Around Town

As predicted, Hannah and her mom stayed home the next morning, but when it was time for lunch, Mary Hayes joined her daughter on a short drive to pick up a couple of plates at Mick's BBQ in the middle of town. "It'll be nice to get out for a bit," Mary said, although she sat in the car as Hannah walked in for a to-go order, having arrived just as the church crowd was being released from their sermons.

"I should have dressed better," Hannah said to herself—comparing her jeans and pullover to the congregants in suits and dresses arriving for barbecue. She was thankful that she was able to tend to her duties without being noticed as a familiar face. After she'd handed her mom the two take-out plates and cranked the car, Mark Daniel's voice came on the air in a promo for his afternoon show: "Tune in at 2 p.m. as we discuss a big cultural shift right here in Wellton on the Voice of the Family with Mark Daniel."

"You listening this afternoon?" Hannah teased her mom on the assumption that this show held little interest for her.

"No, dear. I don't actually care for that program ... the way he does it," her mother confirmed. "I'm afraid he comes across as a little bit self-important. I'm sure that's not what he intends, but I find the tone of these strong opinions to be unpleasant."

Hannah shrugged as she turned to look behind her while

backing out of her parking spot. "I guess self-important is what you'd need to be if you were sure your opinions should be heard by a large audience."

"And his mother, bless her heart, raising him alone like that. It couldn't have been easy on them."

"What happened to his dad? Earl Ford said something about an accident?" Hannah pulled into the street as she waited for her mom's explanation. Mary Hayes wasn't much of a storyteller, but she did piece together a few phrases that drew something of a picture.

"Yes, very sad. There'd been some things going on."

"Like what?"

"Just some things in the family. With his business. He was in a little bit of trouble at work. His car was packed up."

"Are you saying he was leaving? Skipping town or something?"

"Oh, there was some talk after the accident. Which is just very regrettable."

"What kind of talk?"

"Rumors. Terrible ones. And poor old Alice Daniel had to listen to all of that. Just wasn't right. Any of it. So unfortunate."

"Rumors like …?"

"Heavens. The most outlandish things. That he'd taken out a life insurance policy. And it was out on Piedmont late one night. Near the bridge. He ran off an embankment going pretty fast. Didn't even have time to brake, they said. That was another rumor."

"So no skid marks, I guess you're saying? He did it on purpose?"

"I have no idea," her mother answered crisply.

"Anybody else get hurt?" Hannah asked.

"Not as I remember. He wasn't discovered until the next morning. There was a picture in *The Wellton Courier*, of course."

"Of course," Hannah said.

"I probably shouldn't be so hard on that young man, given all that he's been through," Mary said charitably. "A few years ago he was trying to start a religious radio station but apparently lost a bunch of money. So he had to keep doing what he's doing at the Wellton station."

"I see," Hannah said.

"I still am not very fond of his little talk show. I mean, this idea of everybody airing their opinions is really, if you ask me, just a way of being argumentative."

"Indeed," Hannah agreed.

There were two routes from home to town—one direct, one out of the way. The direct one took them past the corner at Southview and Earlie where a tree had fallen on Martin Hayes's car during an afternoon storm. The indirect one took them on a winding road out to Piedmont, where they turned on a highway that headed into town. Hannah had taken the direct route to Mick's BBQ and back, and as they reached that spot again, she gently asked, "Mom, would you prefer that I go the other way next time?"

"Honey," her mother answered, shaking her head, "all the streets have memories. This is the way we go. Let's don't waste our time taking the long way. Let's get home."

"Okay," Hannah said.

CHAPTER 18
Life after Loss

Later that afternoon, Hannah was back at Miss Bertie's—set up with recorder and notepad in the den and ready to listen again. "Miss Bertie," she asked, "you said there was a time when you couldn't 'figure it out.' What did you mean by that? Do you mind telling me about these experiences that sound like they were pretty difficult for you?"

"Well, dearie, I haven't discussed these subjects in a long time, but I'll see if I can rustle them out of my memory." Miss Bertie paused a moment, tapping her fingers on the arm of her chair as she collected her thoughts. Clearing her throat, she spoke again. "First, let me say that I am thankful for my grandfather's resilience—his instinct for survival in a set of wartime experiences that left little in the way of comfort or hope, but just this idea: keep going. And I can't help but wonder, is this a trait particular to my lineage (I'm doubtful), or does the body itself, the spirit of man, have an inborn need to keep going? That's what I've felt."

"You have?" Hannah asked, not sure what else to ask but wanting to prod for more.

Miss Bertie looked upward in reflection. "Oh, yes. There was a time, back all those years ago, I was entirely alone—at least in terms of my own life and where I would go from there. One person. Lost. Searching for the familiar, for hope, for home. It was not unlike those years the locusts had eaten. That's an image from the book of Joel, where you'll find a fine dose of desolation: 'What the locust swarm has left the great locusts have eaten.' Those passages say there was nothing left. The land was empty and devoid of hope. I've seen it myself, figuratively speaking. That's what this poor, sad earth offers up sometimes. But you know what made the whole thing harder? Pretending it never happened. Keeping the secrets of sorrow. That's a heavy undertaking, I can tell you."

Hannah felt a sorrow rise up within as she heard of someone else's terrible days. "I'm sure it's a very heavy undertaking, Miss Bertie."

"You may not be surprised how it was then," the elderly teacher continued. "No one talked about things. Not at bridge club. Not in the teacher's lounge. Or at least I didn't give voice to those experiences. To me, it wasn't right to call attention to my own struggle. That was not the thing to do. Not the way to be. Sometimes, though, I might acknowledge the lost marriage. Especially as divorce got more popular and common."

"I didn't realize you were divorced."

"As a matter of fact, I was. Then I took what I could carry in my suitcases and pursued a new plan. Or, not really a 'plan' so much as I tried something different, unexpected, unusual in those days. I had heard about a teaching job down in Florida. First grade. I applied. I was hired. I moved away, and there I was."

"I assumed you'd always lived in Wellton."

"You might think that because I've been back for so long, but I did take a twenty-five year break. These numbers don't mean much when you're as old as I am. But I returned in '64 to take care of my mother."

"That was the year before I was born," Hannah said, as she tried to run the numbers in her head. Had Miss Bertie been in her early 60s when Hannah sat in her Sunday school class thinking she looked quite ancient? She laughed as she added, "I guess kids don't think anyone had a life before they got here, so by the time you were my teacher, I never thought of you as having a 'before.'"

"Indeed I did. Sometimes all we know to do is separate from the place we're in. I did not do it well, or with courage or conviction. But I did leave," Miss Bertie answered. "Learning the lessons, however, came much slower. That's the problem about leaving. You take yourself with you. You can't escape just by what you do on the outside. The real exit strategies have to start from within."

"Exit strategies?"

"Well, how shall I explain this ... it's easy to fall into traps of sorts, sometimes of our own making. And when I was away, I could see pretty clearly I wasn't the only one who had certain misunderstandings, shall we say. As a teacher sometimes I could see what remained unspoken in the faces of the little children in my classroom. This wasn't from any Union battlefield, like my grandfather had seen. Here, the war zone was the home, the city, the school—really, what was inside them that wasn't being fed love and light."

Miss Bertie paused as she searched her mental filing cabinet for a clearer point, which led to a shrug. "One of my teacher friends said these things are none of our business. Celeste told me more than once, 'We are only concerned about what happens in the classroom, what occurs in front of our eyes. If there's low self-esteem, that's for the families and churches to handle. If someone's parents are getting a divorce or the father lost his job or the mother has an illness—sad as it is—that is not our concern.' That's what Celeste kept saying, but I wasn't so sure. I found the unseen impossible to ignore."

Hannah tried but failed to pinpoint an observation. "The unseen … ?"

"Let me show you what I mean," Miss Bertie said as she pulled herself up to retrieve a framed photograph on the wall.

CHAPTER 19

Seeing Life through a Cloud

"I have photographs in here. Don't we all? But what story do they tell?" Pointing toward the frame, Miss Bertie said, "Look, here I am as a child on the front steps of this very home. This tiny family in a tiny speck of time in the middle of the earth, but to me it may as well have been the whole world."

She handed the frame to Hannah who easily picked out the chubby face and rounding body of a preteen Bertie Dupree. Her mother was also a round lady, and there was her stocky papa and her three stocky brothers.

"Mamma has been gone twenty-five years. That was not a tragedy, per se. She was the age I am now, eighty-five. I was sixty. We couldn't stop this from happening. Nonetheless, many years have passed since I've seen her. Same for Papa, except even longer. When he left, I was twenty-five, and this loss was the first I knew that the world changed when people stopped breathing … the first I knew of waking up each morning into an existence where no Papa lived and only the next world would bring us back together. In more recent years, my brothers have passed as well, and I am the last one remaining, the last one standing. So, let me ask you, dear, is all that came before me just wiped out, as if it didn't exist, as if it's over?"

Like a student being led to her answer, Hannah said, "No?"

Miss Bertie returned to her chair as she continued. "So they've been gone a long time, my parents have and even my brothers, yet I've never been without their influence. Sometimes it's as if they're still here, just in another room somewhere. So, don't you imagine that other children, whether their experiences were good or bad, feel that same kind of influence? The past is still present?"

"Yes, I do," Hannah following the lead to her answer.

"We're surrounded by a cloud of witnesses, the Good Book tells us. And that goes back to my parents and yours, my grandparents and yours, all the way back and back till it all began. So, dearie, mainly what I'm saying is, the unseen has a lot of influence, but you won't always know what that is for someone else."

Hannah tried to keep up with her teacher's words but wasn't sure if this was an old lady rambling or if she should wait out the point. Yet she found a question inside her head that brought the interview back into focus. "Miss Bertie," she asked, "what are the unseen things that influenced your life?"

"Oh, now that is a good question," Miss Bertie answered, "a good question indeed. Certain things trigger memories I don't usually discuss but still have influence. The failure in my marriage brought shame and embarrassment, I assure you—both for me and for those who gently asked or made vague references. Yet that unseen thing pales in comparison to the tenderest loss, a cherished child, my baby, given and taken at the same time. Oh how that hurt, not that I could talk about it. His son, the bearer of his name. He would have never said, 'It's your fault,' but I felt the accusation in the silence—even if that accusation was only coming from my own spirit."

"I'm sorry, Miss Bertie. I didn't know."

"Thank you, dearie. Times were certainly difficult, but I don't have to tell you that. People know now that these experiences are hard. I see these notices in the paper where you can go to meetings and talk about a loss that, in my day, it was best not to mention. But they didn't go away—those feelings—even though, overall, things weren't so bad. Generally speaking. If I looked in one direction—toward desperate poverty in foreign countries or to crime-prone areas in this country—I could see I was doing quite well for myself. However, if I looked toward the neighborhoods I drove through, with all the children running across the lawns, I would remember something was missing."

Miss Bertie sighed. "Comparison is a terrible thing. But knowing so isn't enough to stop doing so."

"Yeah," Hannah said, wincing inside at the number of comparisons that kept her off center herself: not married, no children, small earnings, uncertain career future, then moving on to her lifeless hairstyle, unstylish clothing, regrettable body shape ...

Interrupting Hannah's unspoken listing of inadequacies, Miss Bertie continued, "Then there's this other thing: on any given day, life brings problems. Maybe there'd been a tough day at school. I'd have an interaction with a parent, the principal, another teacher, even a clerk at the grocery store—just someone who had done or said the wrong thing. The words would replay, fester, and grow larger as I came home. The next morning, I would start again. Heading back into the life I knew, I tried to maintain a pleasant demeanor—that was my plan—but there'd be another innocuous interaction. Something would happen, and the secret I held onto would come right back out."

Miss Bertie shook her head in sadness. "I hid a hardened heart—one that fossilized with irritations, annoyance, bitterness. You try to pretend these things aren't there, but they pop up in little incidences. Like that first moment you arrive at school, and you find someone's in your parking place—the one that belongs to you! Or hearing from a parent who completely misunderstood the situation that you had taken great care to resolve. Or getting direction from Central Office that you know is all about appearances and is going to take up your time but won't make a hill of beans of difference.

"Those are the routine things that keep you off center. Then something big happens, and suddenly a battle rages inside your head. I am sorry to say this, but it's true. The worst day, by far, was when I heard that my former husband had become a father to a little girl. First, there was his new wife, and I was thinking, 'Good luck to her.' Then this baby was born, and the news came to me like a dagger to the heart."

Miss Bertie let out a long breath as the memory returned. "How could this be? How dare he go on to new life when I had conceded my own?"

The words fell quiet as the old teacher paused in her remembrance. Moments later, she wrapped up for the day. "I'm sorry, dear, I need to rest now. May I fix you a bite to eat?"

Hannah declined the offer of leftovers from Sunday lunch and thanked her teacher for this story. "I'll be back as soon as I can," she said, although that "soon" would be slightly delayed by the front moving in.

CHAPTER 20

Checking the Weather

A short time later, Hannah returned home to find her mother in the den watching the 24-hour weather station. "This storm's going to be a big one," Mary Hayes said as a forecaster predicted the path of a hurricane churning in the Gulf of Mexico that would be heading toward Wellton by week's end.

"The town will close down," Hannah acknowledged. "But probably not the *Courier*, so I assume I'll be busy."

"My appointment ...," Mary said.

"On Wednesday, yes. I'll take you."

"I know you're busy. I can get there. I just need someone to pick me up when I'm done."

"I'll take you. I'll stay with you."

"I don't want to interfere in your responsibilities," her mother insisted.

"You won't," Hannah insisted in return.

This conversational reassurance did not quell Hannah's unspoken anxiety. Would the storm forecast really be a problem? Would her mom be able to receive her next chemo treatment?

The drumbeat of weather warnings kept the town on edge, while milk, bread, and batteries left the grocery store shelves. The appointment stayed on schedule, however, and as planned, Hannah broke away on Wednesday morning to drive her mother to the infusion center at Wellton Hospital.

The room had a half-dozen recliners for patients and the same number of armchairs for their visitors, yet Mary was the only one being treated that day. A television offered up the latest news stories in the background as Katie Lawrence, a nurse near Hannah's age, attached the chemo drip to Mary's arm. "This part will take about 45 minutes," Katie said. "Are you comfortable? Or comfortable enough?"

"I'm doing fine," Mary answered stoically. "Doing fine."

"Okay, here we go," Katie said to commence the session. As the nurse stepped back, the news switched to a weatherman with a report on the track of Hurricane Opal. "They just scare us to death with all these warnings," she said, shaking her head. "But hospitals don't close, so it doesn't really matter what the weather's like. I'll be here."

"We certainly appreciate all you do," Mary told her.

Katie smiled in return. "I love helping sweet patients like you."

"Did you grow up in Wellton?" Mary asked as Hannah listened to their conversation.

"No, I moved here a few of months ago."

"You like it so far?"

"Sure, it's real friendly."

"Have you found a church home?" Mary brought up the question seemingly required by southern code.

"Not really, but I did get a visit the other day from this couple who said they're starting a new kind of church," Katie answered. "They said it's for people like me ... people who have weird hours and can't get off on Sundays or can't show back up on Wednesdays for church supper ... because I can come on Friday night and wear whatever I want."

"The Eternal Rock church?" Hannah interjected.

"Yeah, that's it."

"Will you go?" Hannah asked.

Katie shook her head. "Probably not, knowing me. It's one thing to say 'that's a good idea.' Actually doing it is another thing."

"Yeah," Hannah agreed.

"The first step's always the hardest," Katie mused. "A lady told me that not long ago."

"A lady?" Hannah repeated.

"Yeah, I didn't know her. A rather large woman. Ran into her at the Piggly Wiggly."

Hannah smiled as she pulled a notebook out of her purse and asked, "You say this was a large woman? Did she happen to give you her name?"

"Yeah, Betty. No, wait, it may have been Bertie. Anyway, I was getting my milk and bread for the storm."

Katie laughed. "My dad always makes fun of people doing that. He says when there's the least little bit of a weather warning, everybody stays home to make milk sandwiches. But I was just doing what people do, what I was told to do."

Hannah made quick notes as her impromptu interviewee described the visit with Miss Bertie in the dairy section. "Anyway, this lady told me there's a land flowing with milk and honey. But she said it's not distant or far away. It's already here. It was nice to think that I've already taken the biggest steps, the really hard ones in getting my degree and my job. I do feel that there's a reason I wanted to do this job. Not just because it's a good job, but because I'm helping people. So Miss Bertie said now that I'm here, I just have to do the thing in front of me. Take the next step, whatever it is."

"Sounds about right," Hannah said as Katie concluded her story.

Sometime later, when the treatment appointment had ended, Hannah pulled her car to a hospital exit door. The sky was gray, and an eerie wind was blowing across the parking lot as she helped her mother into the passenger seat. "Need anything?" Hannah asked.

"No, I'm fine," Mary said. "Let's get home."

CHAPTER 21

Waiting Out the Storm

By the next afternoon, the town had settled in for hours of soaking rain and high winds. Hannah sat with Mary, who mostly stayed in bed resting uncomfortably from the previous day's treatment. "Would you like anything to eat?" Hannah offered more than once. But no, Mary turned her down over and over. This would be a time of waiting it out—both treatment recovery and weather conditions.

The wind whipped against the house, and rain fell hard on the roof even as it spewed sideways against the window panes. The TV stayed tuned to the station in Montgomery reporting conditions all over that part of the state, alerting residents to the damage the hurricane was causing to homes and businesses. Yet here, the occupants waited it out while listening to the torrents bear down.

Sometime during the evening, the sound of a loud boom in the distance broke through the noise of the storm, and the house turned dark.

"Oh … the lights went out," Mary observed quietly.

"Yeah, I guess they did." Hannah lit candles they had kept at the bedside, just in case this happened. Then she waited some more, until near midnight, when the winds died down, and the rain softened. As the world outside turned quiet, Hannah walked down the hallway to her bedroom for a few hours of sleep—wrapped in both relief for the silence and an unsettled spirit about the days ahead.

By the time the sun rose again the next morning, power

was restored—a fact hard to miss when the announcement came in the early hours in the form of lights and TV returning to life. Hannah was quickly in her mother's bedroom to attend to the interruptions.

"Everything okay?" Mary asked as she stirred awake.

"Yes, the power came back on, so I'm turning off everything I missed last night. Which is most things."

Pulling on quick clothes, Hannah stepped outside to check for damage. Leaves, twigs, and other small debris had scattered across lawns and in the roadway, but the house seemed okay. She walked around to the back patio where she could see the stretch of wooded backyards of her neighbors. On one side, Jim Bryant called out from his driveway, "Hannah, y'all alright?"

"Yeah, we're fine," she answered.

"You lose your lights?" he asked.

"They went out sometime around nine. But they're back on now."

"Same here."

On the other side, Walter Douglas called to Hannah from his backyard. "Hannah, you and your mom okay?"

"We are," Hannah answered.

"You get your lights back on?"

"Yes, we lost them about nine last night, but they're back on now."

"Same for us," Walter yelled back. "That was some storm. One of our trees fell, but it didn't hit the house, thank the Lord."

Back inside, Hannah dressed for the day and said goodbye to her mother. "I'm heading to work. I know there will be a lot to do."

"Be safe," Mary said.

"I will."

During the day, Hannah took photos for the paper

and interviewed those who had damage. One lady cried as she talked about losing a home where she had raised her children, though her husband hugged her and said, "It's okay, hon. We're both safe."

Hannah felt both the sorrow and gratitude as if it were being handed directly to her heart, yet she pushed it back, focusing instead on her sentences:

After a night of strong winds and pounding rain, the sun rose again in Wellton on Friday morning. By press time, power had been restored to thousands of homes across Central Alabama though some areas are still experiencing outages. Public schools remain closed, and many businesses have encouraged workers to stay home if travel is deemed unsafe.

When her work was done, Hannah gathered her raincoat and purse and stepped out of the office for the short walk to her car. The rain had receded by now yet the sun was still struggling to dry up the deep puddles in the pavement.

As Hannah splashed noisily to her parking spot, from somewhere nearby, she thought she heard a sound. Somehow, even along the small town's busiest street, a teeny tiny sound caught her attention. The sound was so small it was like half a bird's chirp or one percent of a dog's bark. But she heard it again—a very small meow. She stepped back toward the shrubs that lined the building, and there she saw a soggy orange kitten in need of help.

"Hey, there," Hannah said as she lifted this new furry friend. She wrapped the stressed creature in the rain jacket and placed her in the car. The kitten's meow grew louder all the way home.

Later that evening, after Hannah had returned from the store with litter supplies and cat food provisions, Mary asked, "Do you think we need a cat right now? Is this a good idea?"

"Mom," Hannah explained, "I need a cat right now."

"Then we have a cat," Mary said.

CHAPTER 22

The Spark that Lights a Fire

It took till Saturday for Hannah to get another chance to make a stop at Miss Bertie's. "You have any damage from Opal?" she asked as they sat in the den.

"Just to my nerves," Miss Bertie answered. "This old house was rattling quite a bit, but I'm thankful that we both survived."

Hannah nodded. "Yeah, I talked with some people who lost their home during the storm. Very sad."

"Oh, I'm so sorry to hear that … so sorry. In this world terrible things happen. They surely do. War. Storms. Illness. Not to mention all the things people do to each other out of anger, jealousy, and what have you. Or just plain old meanness. But to lose a home … to be separated from what you've known … it's like losing part of who you are."

Hannah added, "They were thankful to be safe. They both said so. They were standing in their yard looking at all of this scattered debris. But even after all they'd lost, they said they were grateful to be alive."

"That, my dear, is one thing that is so truly beautiful about human resilience … when someone survives a storm, loses so much, and somehow finds the words to say 'thank you.' Can you imagine what it takes to be able to do that? Can you imagine how a human heart has to be designed to allow for this feeling of gratitude to come bubbling up in the face of something really terrible?"

"No," Hannah said, shaking her head. "Not really."

"Well, it's in there. In each of us. It truly is. But the thing is, we didn't put it there. This ability is in our design. I mean, take Jacob, for instance—Esau's twin. He started out as a frustrated, resentful fellow. You know the story."

"Yeah, quite well. I think you told it to me."

"I'm sure I did. But you get my age, and you repeat yourself without hesitation," Miss Bertie said with a wink. "As you know, Jacob had tricked his father into giving him a blessing that, by some ancient rite of passage, was supposed to go to his firstborn brother. The result was that, when this trick was discovered, he lost everything else. His home. His family. He fled for his life, and he was all alone on a difficult journey. Or seemingly so. Because as he was fleeing, he stopped for the night and rested his head using a stone for a pillow. While he slept, he had a dream that showed him he was in the presence of something holy … something divine that he had no words to describe. In that place, in that presence, he felt gratitude. That's what I'm getting to. Is that ability not a miracle in itself—to feel grateful while standing alone in a foreign land, having left behind everything else you've known in your life?"

"I see your point. Somehow, in the midst of a terrible thing, we can feel thankful—and that itself is the miracle?"

"Yes, my dear. My storm was figurative, of course. I fled as Jacob did. But I learned that home isn't always what you think it will be. Home, the literal place, doesn't always bring a good feeling. That's kind of what I was trying to say earlier. These good feelings of blessing, gratitude, optimism, well being—the things that make you feel at home in the world—they begin within and go with you wherever you are. Or else they're missing from within, and you can't find them anywhere. That's what I discovered while I was away."

"Well, Miss Bertie, how exactly did you do that?"

Hannah pressed.

"Now, let me see," Miss Bertie mused as she assessed the points of her next story. "I believe I mentioned Celeste—my teacher friend from those days. In an odd way, an unintentional way, she helped me see the error of my thinking. I'd tell her stories about the days back at home, and she always provided the support I was craving. When I would complain about this thing or that, she would quickly sweep me up in the comfort of her indignation. She was good at that—siding with me completely, placing the blame elsewhere. So reassuring. I can promise you, Celeste knew how to say 'It's someone else's fault' better than anybody. I loved and needed her for that."

Miss Bertie shook her head at the memory. "But I'd left something out of the story. I couldn't tell her about the daughter who wasn't mine. Oh, I tried so many times, but the news would choke in my throat if I started to mention it. So this piece of news stayed inside. As best I recall, the baby was two years old before I finally found the words. School was breaking soon for the summer when Celeste and I had a few last moments in the lounge.

"She pulled out a cigarette and lighter as she asked, 'Going home for a visit, are you?' When I said yes, she followed with her routine well wishes for my trip: 'Hope you don't run into your ex.' That's when I threw the news out there, as casually as I could: 'Well, you know he has a child now, a daughter.'

"The words just sat there for an unbearable moment. So awkward and painful. Celeste gave a one-sided shrug. 'Good thing you got out when you did,' she told me. Then she leaned back, pulled on her cigarette, and blew a long exhale of smoke toward the ceiling. 'That poor girl,' she said, shaking her head. 'She will never amount to anything.'"

Miss Bertie paused and gave a silent shrug. "Celeste meant well. She only intended to reassure me that my choice had been wise. But the indignity of ingesting those words as comforting tonic was too much to bear, even for a woman with hidden bitterness. Instead they created a schism in my heart about the kind of person I wanted to be."

"What'd you do?" Hannah asked.

"Well, with that divided heart, I headed home to visit my mother—and that's when I saw her, this daughter who was not mine. I was in the Piggly Wiggly, actually, in the canned goods aisle. She was standing alone next to her buggy. So small and fragile, a young girl in need of care. When she was in front of me, I could not look away, and something changed inside of me. I didn't know her to talk to her. What could I say as the woman who left her father? As was the case with my grandfather—if he hadn't divorced his wife, I wouldn't be here. If I hadn't left, this child wouldn't have arrived. Yet here she was living in the grace of my terrible days."

"Did you speak to her?"

"Oh, no, that would not have worked. For I only had that split second of seeing her before her mother returned and dropped her cans in the cart. I was not the only one with residual bitterness, I'm afraid. When her mother saw me, she said to her daughter, 'Come on. Let's go.' And they quickly walked away."

CHAPTER 23

In the Aisles of the Mission Field

"So, she knew who you were—the mother did?" Hannah asked.

"This is Wellton, dearie. Everybody knows everybody, or if not in depth, at least they know some little part of a story that has gathered around the individual. And an attitude, a response, a point of view develops."

Miss Bertie shook her head with sadness. "But I didn't forget what I'd seen. I stood there with a moment of gratitude for this new kind of vision. The circumstances in other lives had aligned themselves in such a way that we were on the same earth, experiencing related plights—this daughter and I. Somehow, for some reason, I was able to see that she was not the source of my pain but a motivation for my purpose on this earth. That is the miracle, wouldn't you agree? To be able to see something—or someone— so differently?"

"Yes, it is, Miss Bertie. I do think you're right."

"So I went back to my foreign land, returned to the school where I taught, and I thought of this child often as I maintained vigil over other people's children. Here's what else happened. My eyes watched. My ears listened. My heart softened. Distracted by purposeful work, I slowly became different inside, and everything on the outside got better too. I have to tell you—I didn't do anything at all for this daughter who wasn't mine, wishing her well only in secret, holding out hope only in private. But in hindsight, I'm pretty sure that I recognized the real result. I started again, again. As I accepted this daughter for Whose image she bore, I accepted myself in equal measure, and I got busy with the things that were here for me to do."

"That is quite a story, Miss Bertie."

The old teacher shrugged. "Later, when I moved back home again, I decided that if I ever had another chance to speak to someone at the Piggly Wiggly, I would do so. Time and again, the Lord presents an opportunity so I just follow through whenever that door opens."

"Oh," Hannah said, "so this is why you told a bag boy to go back to school and a bakery chef that she was doing the Lord's work?" Hannah thought for a moment. "And you told that guy in the parking lot to go visit his dad? And that lady who's an artist? She started painting again because you talked in the cereal aisle?"

"Well, my dear, where else should I have done these things? They were there. I was there. The time was right. There was no point in pretending this wasn't my opportunity to make a difference in a child's life. An adult child, perhaps, but someone with a young and yearning heart nonetheless."

The story seemed over. Everything made sense, until Hannah asked another question. "Do you know what happened to that daughter?"

"Just the basics … married, but widowed early, had a child. I'd see her in town now and again with her son. But it wasn't a friendly experience. I could almost imagine that her father dropped my name a time or two with certain distaste, and she probably internalized this point of view. Why wouldn't she?"

Miss Bertie shook her head. "I suspect things weren't easy for her in childhood. My former husband, even in the next marriage, still exhibited some of the same traits of not stepping up to his challenges and of pouring the numbing agents a little too freely. So the daughter left home early for a marriage to a promising young man, but I think there were still issues ... not unlike the ones she'd known."

Hannah offered her own view. "It's so weird, isn't it, that people do the same thing all over again? You think they'd know better."

Miss Bertie shrugged. "It's hard to change the cycles of what is familiar, my dear—for any of us. In the case of this child—Alice—she married a man who ran an electronics shop. He sold radios and TVs, did some repairs, but a bigger place opened up in Wellton, and people went there. He had this grand vision and expanded his store, and mostly that just brought a debt he couldn't pay. 'Bad management will do most anything,' as Manuel would say. Everything just seemed to be collapsing for him, apparently, and then he had a terrible accident. Not really sure what that was about, but there were rumors."

A thought registered with Hannah. "Miss Bertie, did you say that this daughter had a son?"

"Yes, I see him more than I ever saw his mother, as a matter of fact. He's quite active at the church, and I understand that he has some kind of radio show on Sundays. His little girl is in my class this year. She's a dear one, she is."

"Mark Daniel is you ex-husband's grandson?"

"Um hmmm. Isn't it funny how we're all connected? And what a blessing it is for me to be able to see that little Emily each week and to help her learn more about the person she was created to be. I didn't get to do anything at all for her grandmother, but I can do what I can now."

"But ...," Hannah didn't know how to voice her question.

"Yes?"

"Well, I've heard …"

"That Mark Daniel thinks I'm a problem?"

"In a word, yes."

"Dearie, I probably am a problem for Mark Daniel. His grandmother passed her attitude to her daughter, which she passed on to her son. I suspect that something of the blame for what he and his mother felt landed on me. Isn't that often the case? You find someone whose fault it is, and things just make sense. The problem for the young Mr. Daniel is, I'm going to stay in that class until they carry me out. As I've said to others, big as I am, carrying me out is not going to be easy to do."

Hannah nodded as she pulled up a memory. "My dad called his show the Sunday Afternoon Speck-tacular, because people call in who are afraid of the specks in other eyes, but probably, deep in their own hearts, are even more afraid of the logs closer to home."

"Quite so, my dear," Miss Bertie said. "Quite so. It's been that way since the beginning of the world."

CHAPTER 24

The Committee Reconvenes

The next Wednesday, Clyde Buchanan called the committee back to order as a group of Wellton Baptist's finest discussed how to draw new members influenced by a changing culture that wanted church to be like a music video. Or, more to the point, what they were going to do if The Eternal Rock Community Church posed a threat to their attendance numbers.

They'd gathered in a room just off the fellowship hall, carrying into the meeting their trays of poppyseed chicken casserole served over rice with a side of green beans and a roll. "We're here to do our due diligence," Clyde said as the committee met over their midweek fellowship supper. "This church has been serving the Lord for more than a hundred years, right in the heart of Wellton. Our heritage is strong, but that's never enough, is it? We've got to make sure our facilities are adequate for today. Our programming should address the needs of the people in our community."

"What the people need is Jesus," Mark Daniel enthusiastically pronounced. "And this poppyseed chicken casserole, which is delicious," he added with a laugh.

"Amen, brother," Sam Prichard offered loudly.

"Well, gentlemen, no one's going to disagree with that," Clyde responded. "Either of those points. But I think as a church we want to make sure we're showing who Jesus is, if you will. How will people see that they have this need? It's almost like ... I hesitate to use the word ... but advertising. We need to look at what we're advertising."

"Advertising?" This distasteful word had been repeated in the voice of an elderly gentleman by the name of Edward Palmer. "The only advertising we need is the Holy Bible."

A slight redness appeared on Clyde's face. "Like I said, I hesitated to use the word, but it's something we need to think about—how we're sharing the message not just of the Gospel but of, if you will, church membership ... of the need to gather together to learn, serve, give."

"I tell you right now," Edward Palmer continued with what can possibly be described as a fairly surly attitude. "Back in my day, you didn't have to have meetings like this. People just knew to bring their families to church, and the fathers around here were the leaders of these families. Now fathers are just running off and abandoning their responsibilities."

At this point a slight redness appeared on Mark Daniel's face, as if he felt the words had hit a little too close to home. He exchanged his enthusiasm for defense as he said, "Mr. Palmer, with all due respect, some fathers are doing the best they can."

"Yeah, but it doesn't help to have women around here trying to take over the man's authority," Edward Palmer replied. "That is just not how God intended the family to be."

This time Myra Hamilton's face seemed to display the ever-so-slightest shade of red. "Gentlemen," she interjected, "I think we're all on the same page here, and if I may say, all the things we are saying are true. Everyone needs Jesus. We should promote our church so that people will know they can find Him here. And most families around here are doing the best they can. But wouldn't it be nice, if we could show them something better ... that there is a better way to do life than telling them how wrong they are? They will know us by our love, the Bible says."

"Yes, and that is why we are here," Clyde agreed as Myra's words helped the committee refocus its attention. "Last time we mentioned something about the children's department ... taking a look at that, because of how important it is to these families we're trying to reach. Mark, did you have something to add to that topic?"

Mark cleared his throat. "Well, I did express my concern about leaving children in the care of an elderly teacher. So that's something you might want to look at." For some reason, his words were coming out with less certitude than he usually offered, however.

Clyde nodded. "Right, we might want to look at all the ways we're serving our children and families. But telling someone it's time to retire is ... I'm not sure it's part of the committee's role. How would we do that?"

The committee was silent for a moment. "Somebody'd have to talk to her," Mark acknowledged with a shrug.

"Any volunteers?" Myra asked.

The silence returned until Mark spoke again. "Well, you could kind of take a look at the whole department— from bed babies on up so it wouldn't look like you were picking on one person ... like an overall review that wouldn't seem so personal." But he followed his answer with a shrug, as if letting go of any stand he'd intended to take. "If you want to leave her there, though, that's up to you. Or up to the committee."

"You know, it wouldn't be a bad idea to get someone in there with Miss Bertie," Myra acknowledged. "Recruiting a young new teacher or couple to help her could be the solution."

"Well, there you go," Mark said, as if the issue had been resolved and his hands had been washed. "Just get somebody else in there with her."

Clyde turned to recording secretary Maggie Johnson, "Let's put down 'children's program review' and 'additional support' as areas where we should give some attention. I probably need to talk to the pastor about this before we take any actions."

The committee moved on to other areas of concern that were ticked off one by one. And when they concluded their agenda and returned their supper trays to the kitchen, Mark Daniel walked out of the building with a splitting headache. Lately things had been confusing for him. As a matter of fact, his desire to pounce on points had gotten upended by a phone call one evening a couple of weeks back.

Turns out, The Eternal Rock Community Church needed a voice for the local area, someone to help them spread the message of their new congregation, and who better to tap for this volunteer role than the Voice of the Family at the local radio station? That's what the call had been about, and suddenly Mark Daniel's convictions had become uncertain. So, yes, he'd been trying to make things right at Wellton Baptist, to help them become more in tune with where things were going. But what if "going" was what he was supposed to do? Things were just very confusing right now.

When Mark took his seat in his car, his memory was jogged by the sticky note he'd left for himself on the steering wheel. On the ride home, he pulled into the Piggly Wiggly parking lot to pick up a jug of milk, as requested by his wife Jennifer.

CHAPTER 25

The Thaw in the Refrigerated Section

In the church kitchen earlier that afternoon, Miss Bertie had guided Tiffany Taylor, the young new dietician recently hired for Wednesday night suppers, on the proper way to prepare the elderly lady's recipe for poppyseed chicken casserole.

To Miss Bertie's mind, Tiffany was slender as a reed, and hiring a thin cook to serve church supper was certainly an interesting approach to take. However, she did want to help this nervous newbie get off on the right foot. It'd been her experience that church folks can be quite opinionated about food, and if things did not go well at the start, Miss Bertie feared, Tiffany would have no idea what she could be getting herself into.

For Tiffany's part, she had never seen so much sour cream and cream of chicken in her lifetime, but she followed Miss Bertie's instructions to the letter. "They will love it, my dear," Miss Bertie told her. "It has long been a favorite at the church." Happy murmurs of fellowship soon turned Miss Bertie's prediction into a factual account as members sat at long tables covered with white plastic tablecloths for their midweek supper.

When the meal was done, Miss Bertie ambled to her car as other congregants were emptying the building at the conclusion of various meetings and children's programs. Once behind the wheel, she mused to herself, "I believe I'll make that recipe for my friends at the halfway house. They should have a chance to enjoy it too."

That is why, a short time later, she rolled her cart into the refrigerated aisle at the Piggly Wiggly to replenish her supply of sour cream. Just then, a man on a mission grabbed a jug of milk and turned quickly on his heel only to stop in his tracks as he came face to face with the large lady.

"Miss Bertie, hello," a startled Mark Daniel said. "Surprised to see you here tonight."

"Well, good evening, Mr. Daniel. What an unexpected treat to run into you," she replied.

"Same to you," he answered, but with a feeling of slight discomfort. "I'm on a honey-do errand," he said, lifting up the jug as if to reinforce his explanation. "Wife's orders."

"Ah, you're a good man to be so attentive to your household. I have so much enjoyed having your bright Emily in my class this year, and I can tell how much she cherishes her dad ... how her eyes light up as you pop your head in to say 'Let's go.'"

"Well, thank you, Miss Bertie," Mark said accepting a simple comment he did not take lightly. "Family's important to Jennifer and me. I'm blessed for sure."

"Did you know that one of the most beautiful parts about teaching a class of really young hearts and minds is seeing them returned to their families?" Miss Bertie asked. "It's not as if you, as the teacher, are ready for them to go— though confidentially, you can be quite glad for the whole thing to wrap up. But it's knowing that you've had a chance to pour a little sustenance into their tender hearts, and they're taking that sustenance back to their families and to their lives. Truly, who knows how long it will stay with them?"

"That's got to be a good feeling," Mark acknowledged.

"Oh, yes. Do you not remember stories you heard as a child? I do—sometimes better than the ones I hear as an adult. In childhood, when you hear a story from the

Bible—just a simple story—you don't have to wonder if it's true, or if it's still relevant for today. You just take it in and store it in your little heart and soul."

"Yes," Mark said, although he didn't know what other point to make and wasn't sure how else to respond, so he just sort of fell uncharacteristically quiet.

"When I began teaching children, a verse popped out to me, right there in Hebrews 5," Miss Bertie continued. "I needed someone to teach me the elementary truths of God's word all over again. I needed milk, you might say, not solid food. What a gift this has been to me, to learn about God in the eyes of those hearing all of this for the first time."

"That does sound like a gift," Mark said, with his heart seeming to soften beyond the old lady in front of him but also to what was stirring within.

"Just seems to me," Miss Bertie said as she placed a large container of sour cream in her cart, "if you want to change the world, a child's heart is the best place to start."

"So it is, Miss Bertie. So it is," Mark agreed as he shifted his jug of milk to the other hand. He was ready to leave, but his feet felt a little like lead at the moment, and he couldn't find a way to make a quick break.

"You just really don't know what these kids are going to be dealing with in the days to come," Miss Bertie continued. "They seem okay now, you know? They're from good families that bring them to church, but that's not a protection from the world around them, is it? They'll still have struggles. As we all do."

"Yeah, that's part of it, for sure," Mark said.

"Now your Emily, she has a question mark in her eyes, and that's a wonderful thing to see."

"A question mark?"

"Oh, that's my way of deciding who's what in a room.

A punctuation review. Think of it this way: Children who carry a question mark—that's a good thing. They are curious. They want to learn and grow. When you see the question mark, it's exciting and shows how much they're willing to absorb, discover, even share. That's your Emily."

Mark smiled. "Sounds right."

"Then there are children with an exclamation point—they're a bit of trouble, they are hard to keep in line. Still, you can see something good ahead. Messy, bold, creative, fun. You're not sure how this will go, but you can sure bet they won't be sitting still during their lifetimes. You'll know which room they enter, for sure."

"An exclamation point ... that was probably me, unfortunately for my mom," Mark said with a laugh.

"I'm sure it was," Miss Bertie said, returning a smile. "Then there are children who live as a comma—they have this pause going on. They're not sure where things are going, so they need to hold back, evaluate, reassess, proceed with caution. They are watching for the next part of the sentence, the next piece of information. They wait."

Mark nodded. "Sounds like my wife. A comma. She doesn't rush into things, but really thinks about stuff."

"But there are also children where it's as if you can see a period being placed on their young lives. These are a concern. They have stopped. Quietly. Succinctly. They are at a stopping point before they begin. Nothing coming in. Not light. Not love. They can break your heart as you see them now, or, one sad day, they can cause you to bolt your doors at night."

Mark nodded somberly and thought of a man this description brought to mind. Someone who quit, who gave up.

Miss Bertie continued, "I can't do much about all the things that happen in the world, but if I can help a few children right now ... help them store up good news they can call on when they have bad days ... well, that is a work worth doing. And that, Mr. Daniel—that's why the children's department is so exciting. If you want to change the world, teach the elementary truths. Give them milk, and who knows where they will go from here."

Mark was nodding again as he took a breath to address the points that had been raised. But he exhaled instead and kept his thoughts to himself. "Speaking of milk," he said switching subjects, "I best get home and get this in the frig. Jennifer's waiting."

CHAPTER 26

Hannah Seeks Clarification

Hannah was at the window in her bedroom, tugging to get it open. It'd always been a struggle for her, with so many coats of paint over the years causing it to stick and making it hard to raise. She was thankful to have her dad's hand there to help her lift. His presence felt so real. But they'd only gotten it an inch or two above the frame when he disappeared into the unseen scenes of a dream, and she opened her eyes into the sorrow of a grief remembered.

An orange cat bearing the name Opal pawed at the bedspread as Hannah reached to pet her new furry friend. Opal stood and lifted her tail as the purrs began, then she turned and pushed her head back under Hannah's hand.

"If you'd just let me pet you, I could pet you," Hannah explained. "You don't have to move around to keep up with my hand." Opal wasn't listening. She pawed again at the bedspread, as if to give instructions for this October day at mid-morning.

"Okay, I'm up," Hannah said.

Soon, she was in the kitchen pouring a bowl of cat food for Opal and a bowl of cereal for herself. As she did, she noticed through the window that Mary was walking in the backyard.

"Mom," she called as she stepped outside with her cereal, "do you need any help?"

"No, sweetie, I was just checking on things," Mary said as she returned to the patio. "Fall's a good time for planting trees and shrubs, and I wondering if anything was missing out here that we should add. Just doing a little surveying, that's all."

"Okay," Hannah said. "But let me know if you're going to do anything. Like digging. I'll help."

"Thank you, sweetie. I will. I certainly will."

Hannah nodded, though with a suspicion that Mary wouldn't actually let her know. She half expected that one day she would look into the backyard and see her mother holding a shovel in one hand while pulling an IV pole in the other.

"The weather is nice, isn't it?" Mary asked. "So lovely this time of year."

"Yes," Hannah said, adding, "I think I'll take a walk, if you don't need me right now."

"Good idea, sweetie. I'm fine here. You enjoy."

Hannah emptied her bowl of cereal, then returned it to the kitchen before changing into walking clothes. She grabbed a notebook and her recorder for her pockets, just in case Miss Bertie was available, then headed out into a bright morning where beams of sunshine warmed her face.

Step by step Hannah walked past the homes in her old neighborhood on Evergreen Drive to make the turn onto Southview, and a few houses later, she was at her elderly teacher's home. She headed toward the backdoor, and once on the stoop she could see Miss Bertie sitting at the kitchen table studying her notes for the next day's lesson.

"Well, my goodness gracious, what a delight to see you this morning," Miss Bertie said when she heard Hannah's knock. "Please come in and join me right this instant. May I warm you a cup of coffee? I still have some in the percolator on the stove."

"No, thanks, Miss Bertie. I took a chance that you'd be here and thought I'd stop by for another visit. Am I interrupting anything?"

"A welcome interruption it is. Please have a seat."

As Hannah pulled out a chair, Miss Bertie said, "You know, you've let me talk so much about myself on all these visits. But tell me, dear, how you are getting along? Are you enjoying your work at the *Courier*?"

"It's okay. It's a job. I'm not doing much more than sitting in city meetings and taking notes, but it's okay."

"Was this what you envisioned for yourself?"

"Oh, no. This isn't it at all."

"What would you do if you could do anything?"

"My dream? I guess that would be ... I think it'd be amazing to write profiles of interesting people. You know, for a magazine like *The New Yorker* or something similar, but ...," Hannah shook her head. "It's just a pipe dream. I'm here. It's there. I don't see how it could happen."

"Is there something in your way?"

"Distance, for one thing. And, I guess ... fatigue at just the very thought of it all." Hannah shook her head. "It's like ... it's like I don't have the energy it would take to reach it. I don't have the fuel I'd need. The resources, you know?" She shrugged. "It's just too far away."

"Oh, I don't know, dearie. If that's your dream, there must be something in it that's already here, that's already close by. Obviously you could leave, or you could stay. Either option is fine, but what I've learned is that you can start doing what you're called to do wherever you are."

"I think that's what I've been discovering," Hannah said uncertainly. "Over the last few weeks I've talked to some people who've been influenced by you, and one by one, I can see that they're all really interesting people, and they're doing something important—each one of them."

"Is that right?" Miss Bertie asked, pleased with this news.

"Oh, yes, but you wouldn't know it right away. You wouldn't realize a janitor has big plans or a baker is doing the Lord's work. But when you listen to ordinary people, you can actually hear that their lives are quite extraordinary."

"Maybe there is something in this that is calling to you?"

"I guess so." Hannah shrugged. "When I was a kid, I wanted to be a preacher. Obviously that didn't work out. Because women preachers," she laughed, "that's just not really happening around here. But I learned more about the church too since then. Really eye-opening things about the ugliness that it's supported—like slavery for heaven's sake. Or segregation. Even churches voting not to allow black members. It's just ... I don't know. It's hard to make all that gel."

"Indeed," Miss Bertie said. "I was ten years old when women got the right to vote, but believe me, the church fought hard against it. People didn't think it was fitting for women to take such matters into their own hands."

"Yeah, but it's like the same voices who said they could decide who was a slave, who said women couldn't vote, who said people of other races couldn't go to their schools or churches are the ones saying women can't be preachers. So, I don't know, I just figured I'd do something else. Because why would anyone want to go to a church like that?"

"Ah, that is a large question. Very large indeed. I'm not quite sure how to answer, except ..." Miss Bertie paused as she seemingly pulled together an impromptu Sunday school lesson for her guest. "The verses where Jesus talks to the woman at the well are some of the sweetest in scripture. Do you know these? The exchange starts out as one of those serendipitous conversations between two people. She's just a woman, someone who has had a number of difficulties, someone getting through a regular day. A seemingly ordinary man speaks to her in the middle of the ordinary task of getting water for her household. Though there are cultural prohibitions challenged by this exchange, she doesn't run away or become offended. She stops to listen, and she asks questions, and after this long one-on-one conversation, she leaves that encounter with a new story to tell."

Hannah nodded, asking, "Is this the part where you say 'go and do likewise?'"

"Yes," Miss Bertie smiled, "but I know it's not easy. Church can be an awkward fit sometimes. My grandfather could have told you about that as well—because he actually got kicked out for not meeting expectations. Does that story sound like one you'd find of interest?"

"It certainly does."

"Let me see if I remember it correctly ..."

CHAPTER 27

A Committee Decision Gets Appealed

"By the time my papa and his sister were born, Manuel ran a store on the land he and my grandmother occupied, and he'd built a house for his new family," Miss Bertie explained. "It was the usual sort of place for those post-Reconstruction days. Logs as walls, dog trot, fireplace, and an upstairs loft where the children slept. They were part of a community—had friends and all that—and sometimes in the evenings, folks would come to visit. Now, Manuel was known to enjoy a little taste of liquor here and there, and he would get carried away. He'd forget himself, and during these festive evenings, he would get the bright idea of showing off his children.

"Let me tell you, Manuel loved his older daughter, Aunt Adelaide—the one he didn't get to see while he was away. Yet he was absolutely smitten by these young new kids, the ones who came during his second chance at life. He wanted to brag about them and put them on display. So, even though they were asleep, he would climb up the stairs to the loft, rouse them out of bed, and bring them down for his guests to admire.

"As you can quite imagine, my papa didn't like being presented in this way. It's easy to see why that would be the case. He was embarrassed, and he felt that alcohol was why this was happening. Therefore, when he was grown, he did not drink alcohol for that very reason.

"Papa was quite serious about taking the good and the bad from this man he loved. We all have to do this, you know. See the good and the bad and decide what part will have the greater influence. It doesn't always work out, obviously. Sometimes we just hit repeat and do the same thing over again. But most of us like to believe it's possible to be who we were created to be and not become the next generation of the very same thing.

"In any case, back to my point. It seems this sipping habit of Manuel's came to the attention of the good folks at his church. In these days, the 1870s or so, they took church discipline quite seriously. For example, if you missed church three Sundays in a row, you could get excluded unless you apologized and promised to attend regularly. Or if rumors got around that you'd been playing cards, a committee would meet and send out someone to investigate. If you wanted to stay in fellowship, you would have to repent and say you wouldn't do that anymore.

"Of course, getting drunk was frowned upon as well. That is the word that reached the church about Manuel. A committee investigated his behavior, they took a vote, and he got excluded from the church."

"Wow, I didn't realize that could happen—an excommunication of sorts," Hannah said. "What'd he do?"

"Interestingly he fought back, in his own way. For all its flaws, people actually need the church—they need community that has love as its principle if not always as its practice. So congregants might get mad at the committees, but they want to get right with the church, or, at the very least, they want a church that's right for them. Manuel petitioned for reinstatement. The committee reconvened to consider his apologies and promises, and I'm sure quite a discussion ensued. Not everyone was on board with the decision, but Manuel had enough support to get back in, and he was re-baptized."

"How odd," Hannah said. "Can you imagine something

meaning so much to you that you would go to that trouble—that you'd make a case for reinstatement to a place that said you weren't good enough?"

"Yet here's another pertinent factor. Once Manuel had been restored as a church member in good standing, he asked for a letter saying so. He wanted the documentation. Back then, if you had a letter that said you were a member in good standing of your current church, you could leave that church and go to another one and present your letter. They would have to take you in on the basis of that letter."

"Sounds sort of like he was getting a passport—he could go somewhere else, having cleared his name, so to speak," Hannah said.

"In theory, but that's not quite the way it went. The point is, this letter gave Manuel power over his church membership. If a committee had ideas about excluding him again, he could simply take his letter and go somewhere else. I do admire that about Manuel—his foresight to wrest control of his church membership from a committee and place it in his own hands. But the other thing is, he never left. He stayed till the very end. He did have his fallback, however, in case he needed to enact an escape clause."

"Oh," Hannah said. "He stayed."

"Yes, dear, and that's really the point I'm making. You can go, or you can stay, as the Lord directs. In any case, I am quite familiar with the underbelly that can show up in a human organization—even one in such a noble pursuit as the work of the church. But think of it this way. It's not just about going to church. It's about being the church. It's about taking it with you."

"Like to the aisles of Piggly Wiggly?"

"Like those very aisles."

Miss Bertie looked toward the sun poking its beams through the kitchen window. "The life I knew ended in

1939," she said in ambivalent tone. "I reached out and reached up for resurrection, and little by little, the feeling returned to my feet, my hands. My heart began beating again at a normal pace, and here I have been ever since. As a matter of fact, you could call this my grace period—that period through which I lived after everything was over, that the grace of God made possible. So, all I would say is, do not let those who disappoint you cause you to forget that you have work to finish. Go or stay, as the Lord directs. But do the thing you are called to do. Become the person you are intended to be."

Hannah felt a warmth of affirmation as she said, "Thanks, Miss Bertie. Hearing your story has been helpful." She shook her head. "I really do wish ..." She shrugged. "I wish I could talk to my dad."

"My dear, that is the longing of so many a daughter walking through this troubled world, is it not? I feel that way myself, even now." Miss Bertie brought back another memory as she added, "My Aunt Adelaide and I talked about that one time. She's the one Manuel had left behind in Wessobulga when he was at war. You remember he'd mentioned her in his letter?"

"Right, there was a daughter."

"She told me that in those years he was away, she waited for him. In the evenings she would stand at the window and look for him. At the same time, he was always thinking about her too—this dear daughter. I could almost see her at the window and him on his cot in camp, separated by so many miles."

Hannah nodded as she took in the image. "Speaking of that letter," she said, "I'd like to use it in the story I'm writing, the one based on all these interviews. Do you mind if I type out a transcript?"

"Take it with you and bring it back later when you're done."

"You're okay with that?"

Miss Bertie shrugged, "What good is an old letter if it isn't shared?"

CHAPTER 28

Moved to the Head of the Class

In another part of the town, some other decisions were also being made. The night Mark Daniel took the milk home to his wife Jennifer, he'd told her about an idea he had. He was the one who was impulsive; she was the one who thought things through. Before he went too far afield, he wanted her counsel on whether this idea was as crazy as he imagined.

As they talked, Mark said, "Sometimes I feel like I'm trying to be my mom's defender and my dad's redeemer. I want to do the right thing that represents them well. But what if that's not really the battle that was meant for me?"

A few days later, they talked again, and, turns out, Jennifer could see it just like he did. This was a really good idea, she said. Surely the hand of providence was on the move.

So the next day Mark called the person who'd reached out to him from Eternal Rock to thank the church for considering him for their media committee. But, at this point, he was going to decline. "Never say never," he said, "but just not right now."

That next Sunday, when Mark and Jennifer brought Emily to the church classroom, he lingered in the doorway. "If you don't mind, Miss Bertie, we'd like to stick around," he said.

Jennifer added, "Yes, Emily talks about you all the time—and all the things she's learning in here. We'd like to see how special it is."

"You are welcome here anytime," Miss Bertie said. For her part, Emily beamed as she entered with her two guests.

Once there, they could see it even more clearly, and that's how Mark and Jennifer Daniel decided to teach in the children's program at Wellton Baptist Church. The first-grade room specifically. It was an awkward fit at first, considering that Miss Bertie usually wanted to do the lesson herself, but, from time to time, she relented and gave one of them a chance to tell the story to the children.

Emily was thrilled that her mom and dad were coming to the class, and she grew in the fear and admonition of the Lord during those months as well as in the years to come. One day, she too would wander onto her own battlefields and find her way back home.

After the time she'd spent with Miss Bertie, Hannah began writing about her elderly teacher's encounters. She filed a series of stories for *The Wellton Courier* about how one person can make a big difference in small ways, and she turned it into a book called *Miss Bertie Explains the Beginning of the World*.

At long last, she had found the story she wanted to tell.

A New Song

Hannah had one other thought that wouldn't let go. She kept coming back to Miss Bertie's grandfather who'd left behind a daughter he never forgot, and the daughter who'd watched for him. "What about her, and me, and all the others who are always missing someone?" Hannah wondered to herself.

Her mind wandered back to what Miss Bertie had told her about the daughter watching from the window in Wessobulga for her father's return. This longing felt so familiar. Sometimes Hannah missed her dad so much her heart ached for one last message. She knew she wouldn't find it here, not on this earth, but she did pour that feeling into a song of remembrance that concluded her book.

The Father's Lullaby

He lay on a cot in camp, feverish and ill, wondering what his missteps would mean to his little girl. He couldn't have loved her more if he had pulled out his heart and handed it to her with his last breath. But he was here, and she was there.

That night in camp, sick unto death, he thought of this dear daughter, and in his grief, a mournful plea eased slowly from his broken spirit:

In my mind, I see you there
And everywhere

A mirage of memory
That never goes away
Be assured
I did not leave
You are not gone
We are together, still.

Far away from this battlefield, his daughter awakened from unsettled sleep. A celestial light peeked through an open window, and she felt welcomed by the sight. The moon had always been her friend—steady, quiet, and present on any dark night.

The loft was warm this evening. Throwing off her cover, she rose, looked out, and looked up as the stars blinked their greeting. The land was still, the night air did not move. In this moment all her own, she opened her heart to distant thoughts as a melody that only she could hear floated down from the heavens:

Sleep, my child, in comforted pose
Dream, my child, released from your woes
For love is greater than fear
Whenever your heart draws near
To hear your father's lullaby

She had heard these words before. They were stored in long ago memory, but sometimes in quiet moments found their way into her waking hours. The melody continued:

Stand firm in the face of any dismay
Journey on in the light of the one true way
The battle is not your own
You know you're never alone
When you hear your father's lullaby.

She took these words in as a treasure beyond what her eyes and ears or mind could comprehend, and as the melody moved around and settled within her spirit, she said with a sigh to the endless sky, "Thank you for this song."

Two hundred miles away, the cot that held her father sagged from the weight of his helpless estate. He could not move. Even so, his feverish mind stirred up the strength of a love that would not end, and he found the breath to voice his deepest plea:

I was born into the life I knew
During these terrible days
Everywhere I look, I see
Others just like me
Each person here
Misses someone there
If I do not return home,
Do not believe that I left
We are together, still
My love was real,
Always.

In the distance between them, his daughter bid farewell to the moon and stars, as she voiced her prayer into the sky: "Take care of those we love, this night and always." And she returned to her bed, where she gathered herself in peaceful slumber.

Remember the Former Things

I come from a long line of old people. My father was older when I was born, my grandfather was older when my father was born, and my great-grandfather was older when my grandfather was born. That's how I ended up at my particular age having a great-grandfather who was a Civil War veteran.

Manuel Harrison Lamberth served in the Confederate Army during the Civil War. Early in his years away, he wrote a letter home. I incorporated that letter in this story as if it had come from Miss Bertie's grandfather. Miss Bertie is a work of fiction. However, the stories she tells about her grandfather are drawn from stories my cousin Grady Lamberth told me about my great-grandfather.

That's one part of how this work came into being.

I thought about the young daughter back at school in Wessobulga. I understand that she and Manuel stayed in touch upon his return, and that her wedding was at his house. But I thought, in any case, about these early years of her life—that sense of wondering where he was and if he would ever return.

That leads to another part of how this work came into being. Manuel said for the reader of the letter to write to his daughter. It's sort of like when Paul writes in scripture "pray for me." What do you do with a request like that when he's been gone from this earth for a very long time? So I wondered, if I could, what would I write to that daughter?

Over the last several years, I tried other versions of a teacher who told stories similar to these, but the manuscripts didn't quite work until I ended up at Miss Bertie. She was the one who could carry this story forward. She helped me write the letter to the daughter of Wessobulga. Or, in a sense, she helped me write a letter I would write to my younger self if such a thing were possible.

There's another part to this story as well. In 2005, I introduced Hannah Hayes to the world through my novel *Life with Strings Attached*. I didn't know how to tell or what to say in a second story about Hannah until Miss Bertie led me back to Evergreen Drive in Wellton, Alabama. I am thankful to her for helping me find home once again.

— Minnie Lamberth

Discussion questions are available at minnielamberth.com

ACKNOWLEDGMENTS

As to this specific work, I would like to thank my fellow Huntingdon College alumni Cindy Bryan, who provided valuable editorial services, and Alecia Glaize, who helped me with my discussion questions. I'm grateful as well to long-time friend and colleague Slats Slaton, who designed the cover. In addition, my coaching group led by Susan Miller and joined by Cyncie Winter and Susan Bruck provided steady support as I developed this story and other creative projects, and my friend and colleague Jason Otis provided ongoing technical assistance. Creativity coaching programs led by Jill Badonsky have also been quite helpful.

More broadly, I've been influenced by the teaching, encouragement, and friendship of many people over many years through my membership at First Baptist Church in Montgomery, Alabama. These influencers include Donna Hoomes, who has taught me so much about teaching children and providing a space for them where church feels like a happy place to be. In addition, when I was the age that Hannah is in this story, Donna McConnico was the staff minister who opened the doors to a church community and encouraged my writing.

I'm also grateful for the abiding support of special friends, such as Jan Bigham Gill and Ellen Haulman, and an extended family for whom humor and love are closest of kin.

ABOUT THE AUTHOR

Minnie Lamberth is the author of *Life with Strings Attached*, winner of the Paraclete Fiction Award, and *Min at Work*, a memoir of her work experiences that has since evolved into a coaching series called *"How to Pursue Your Creative Purpose."*

Since 2000, she has been a full-time writer helping clients craft their marketing messages or create their writing products. She lives in Montgomery, Alabama.

Visit *minnielamberth.com* to learn more.